NORMAL?

STEPHEN J. MULROONEY

Busterfly
Kansas City, Missouri

Busterfly

Kansas City, Missouri

Copyright©2012 by Stephen J. Mulrooney

First Busterfly edition 2013

Busterfly and Busterfly logo are trademarks of Busterfly LLC
Printed in the United States of America
ISBN 978-0-9889928-4-9

Dedication

This book is dedicated first and foremost to the great love in my life, my husband, Jerome P. Van Wert, whose love and support make all things seem possible. This daydream of a knight kept me on the quest to finally sit down and write, and if you look, you will find him in every expression of love in the story.

The book is also dedicated to Adelaide and Frank Mecevitch, who became my extended family a decade before I met Jerome, and have remained so ever since. They never stopped believing that I was a writer, even though it took over thirty years to prove them right.

Finally, this book is dedicated to my sisters Regina Mulrooney and Dorothy J. Hamernik, and our extended family on both sides for their love, support and belief in what I was trying to accomplish; and to all the furry members of our family who have, do and will always inspire me through their limitless and unconditional love.

Acknowledgements

This story has been floating around in my mind for over three years. In all that time, the wonderful people you are about to meet kept haunting me to bring their story to life so that you would someday know them. They never stopped believing that we would all one day be real. Congratulations guys, we made it.

I would also, however, be remiss if I didn't offer a very special thank you to Elizabeth Andersen and Madeleine Hogan for their editing skills, Jamie Rich and Antonio Mirás Neira for their assistance with the cover design, Clark Kenyon for cover layout and text composition, Patrick Wang for his inspirational words of encouragement, Miss Jackie Silberg for all her advice and support, and Jordan Ashley Hocker for the poem about: "Having the Inspiration" that unblocked the writer's block.

I hope that you enjoy reading this book as much as I have enjoyed writing it.

Prologue

Were it a dream, it would be a most wondrous dream; but it's more. It's a life. And I don't have to remember any of it. It remembers me.

I rely heavily on life's memory, because I don't seem to remember much myself these days. I guess that's normal. When you're busy making memories, there is little time to recall them.

Fortunately, not all memories need to be recalled. They have no past because they are always present. They are the present you give yourself every day. They are ever a part of you, and never apart from you. You live and wear them proudly, and you wouldn't change them if you could.

My interactions with my family are such a wardrobe. I wear them daily, and would feel completely naked without them. I constantly find that they clothe my thoughts, my words, and probably every bit of good that I've ever done in my life. In any given situation, I inevitably find myself channeling one member of the family or another, and always for the better. No other channel gets better reception. To understand me, you would have to know and understand them.

I mention this because just recently an ex-boyfriend, a mistake that didn't wait to happen (we'll bridge that cross when we get to it), suggested that I write a story about my family. "Your family –actually you and your entire family

– are far stranger, and certainly a whole lot more interesting, than any of the so-called fiction that you have written
so far."

"Let's face it," he added rather sarcastically, "you and
your family are not exactly what anyone would call normal. Actually, you're all more like the antonyms of normal. Just pick an antonym, any antonym in the dictionary
to the word normal, and there's bound to be a picture of
some member of your family next to it. As a matter of fact,
if I tried to define any of you, I would probably fare better looking through comic books for some surreal pop-up
characters, or maybe pop-up caricatures."

And, just to make sure that he drew enough blood, he
added, "The best part is that even if your writing isn't very
good, the subject matter has got to be far more interesting
than anything you've done so far. It's almost like a win-win
situation. Wouldn't that be a nice change?"

Considering the source, or is it the sores, the intended
slap did little more than awaken something wonderful inside me. And instead of getting angry or upset, I smiled
and thanked him. He had intended to drop a bomb. He
dropped a balm instead. He was right. My family and I
are probably not normal by definition, but rather than
abnormal, we exceed the definition; we're more like su-
pernormal.

Normal implies sameness, conformity, and freedom
from any trait or characteristic that would make you
unique or exceptional in any way, much like a Republi-
can housewife, or my ex-boyfriend's criticism. We don't fit

the mold. As Mother would say, "There is nothing moldy about us."

Mother, who is obviously fond of sayings, is fond of saying, "Life is a cupboard of spice; let every slice of it change with the seasonings. Be anything you want to be, but please don't be bland or normal. Normal is actually something distasteful and unnatural; it's like your father's cooking."

None of us are like my father's cooking. We are all tastefully extraordinary and interesting. We've all managed to avoid hopping on the bland wagon. I'm proud that we've accomplished that; as a matter of fact, I'm proud of everything about us.

And, it is for that reason that I agreed with Bryan, the ex. I should write a story about my family – all of us. What a novel idea! (Of course, if I was bitchy, I'd probably say that it was the only one he's ever had, or at least put it in parentheses.)

So with the kind permission of my entire "not so normal" family, the following story is offered with as much truth and *honesty* as any fictional character could possibly deliver.

One

My family seems to have a knack for amusing names. Take the hyphenated surname of my parents, who are actually my uncles, Ben Poole and Tom Hall. Poole-Hall would have been a difficult enough last name to live with. But my given name is Gene, just Gene. That leaves me with Gene Poole-Hall. It sounds like some *Wheel of Fortune* puzzle answer, doesn't it?

I was barely four when my uncles adopted me into their lives. Naturally, I called them both uncle and by their first names, Uncle Ben and Uncle Tom. For obvious reasons, that didn't sit too well with them. That would have been the case even if we didn't live in an ethnically mixed neighborhood. So, Uncle Ben insisted on being called Mother, which was the nickname that most of his friends called him anyway. Uncle Tom, Mother's life partner, became Dad because, well, it just somehow seemed to fit both him and the family situation.

Mother, by the way, calls me Genie, not Gene, and fortunately he's the only one who does. I think he started doing it so that he could embarrass me by humming the *I Dream of Jeannie theme* song every time I entered a room … which he still does.

Mother and Dad had been together more than ten years when Mother's sister, Anna – my mom – passed away. Mother insists that I say passed away instead of died when I speak about my mom or anyone else who has, you know, passed away, because, "Passed away implies that there is still more to follow, as when someone says 'That's all I want to say about the subject.' Died has this morbid, 'nothing to look forward to' ending that you only find in a politician's promises or your Aunt Allie's jokes."

I must admit that I don't really remember my mom, or when she passed away. She had been sick a long while, and I didn't get to see her much during that time. Sadly, she has slowly faded from the photos of my life. Any memories of her that there might have been have somehow slipped away.

I wish that I remembered her more. She often seems like the nicest person I never met. Mother and Dad have tried to keep her memory alive by telling me stories from their early times together. But these stories are like old postcards from a time long gone. They are from someone else's trip, not mine. My trip, my life, my lasting memories begin with Mother and Dad.

Dad's an enigma to most people. He's a bit of a chameleon. His life appears very different when viewed from an unknowing distance, not unlike one's view of a Van Gogh painting, or a drag queen, which, by the way – considering their colorful layers – are actually very similar.

Outside the environ of the family, Dad would probably seem to be a somewhat typical Wall Street businessman who loves sports, mixes well, and is probably having too much fun to have met the right woman. The truth is that he's so much more. The reason he is having so much fun is because he met Mother, who was anything but the "right woman" – except, of course, at work, where Mother was any and every woman he wanted to be.

Mother is proof that actors speak louder than words. He was already a famous female impersonator by the time I came to live with him. He had become the main attraction in a popular drag show at the Kit Kat Club, as well as a mentor and guide to the rest of the performers in the troupe … hence, the nickname Mother.

Mother has always believed that a waist is a terrible thing to mind. Because of his hefty size and love of big cars, he chose suitable stage names like "Minnie Van" and "Winnie Bago," before reducing a little and eventually settling on a more form-fitting "Mary, Mother of Gaud." "I was initially going to go with the name 'Anna Rexia,' but just as a gag," Mother often jokes. "And once, I even tried the name 'Liz Turine,' but that was too hard to swallow."

Mother's impersonations, like everything else he does, were always audio and picture perfect. He focused mainly on full-figured performers so as to capture and exhibit the full feeling of each impersonation. He did, however, become most famous for his impersonation of a rather large

Cher in a skimpy corset, which he always introduced with, "What, haven't you ever seen anyone retain water before?" And after a proper pause, "Welcome to Lake Erie!"

He also did the most hilarious "Shirley Temple of Doom" number, where the three hundred pound little Shirley flattened an entire zoo while singing and dancing "Animal Crackers in My Soup."

The other members of the drag show troupe, Mother's co-stars, were a very close-knit group who quickly became part of his and Dad's extended family, and eventually part of mine.

Aunt Sue, the oldest and longest-running member of the troupe, performed as "Sue Shee, the Japanese Treat." No one knows Aunt Sue's real name, it's changed so often, but he's black, not Japanese. Mother claims not only is Sue more trick than treat, but also, the closest he's ever been to Asian is Chinese takeout.

Aunt Allie also likes to tease him about his supposed Asian heritage by referring to him with an affected accent as "my Aging friend."

Aunt Allie was known as "Allie Kat, the Persian Kitty." Aunt Allie's real name is Ali Bashir, and he really is Persian from Iran. Mother says that Aunt Allie has always been too much of a real girl to be a legitimate drag queen. "They just got his plumbing order mixed up. He doesn't need to act; he just needs to dress better on stage."

The truth is that Aunt Allie would remind anyone of bumbling Aunt Clara on *Bewitched*. Aunt Sue thinks that Allie's bumbling is mostly a language problem. "They haven't invented a language that he understands yet. The poor thing hasn't even figured out why there are so few cars in autobiographies."

And finally, there was Aunt Kaye who performed as "Kaye Sera, the Whatever Girl." I don't remember him much either. Aunt Kaye passed away soon after I arrived. Mother often refers to him as "the pick of the glitter." To me, unfortunately, he's just another beautiful postcard.

There is one other member to our extended family, who is not a member of Mother's troupe, but who is perhaps the family's most important addition. It is Uncle Josh, Mother's lifelong best friend, and for a long time the romantic object of his romantic affliction.

Uncle Josh is a well-respected rabbi, and in every way a member of the family long before there ever was one. His relationship with Mother is a story unto itself. And so, as their story is the beginning of all that is to follow, let's begin there.

As Mother would say, 'It's better to begin at the beginning anyway. It's so much less confusing than beginning in the middle, and a lot longer than beginning at the end."

Two

Ben, aka Mother, and Josh couldn't be any closer if they were twins. Mother says, "We would have been like those cute little Asian Mothra twins, if I wasn't the size of Mothra when I was born."

Ben and Josh were actually born minutes apart (Josh is less than a half hour older) in the same hospital to mothers who lived in the same run-down Lower Eastside apartment building, or as Mother calls it, "the really flat." As the only children in the building outside of Josh's and Ben's older sisters, they were destined to become close friends, despite being predestined for very different destinations.

Josh's parents were Jewish, financially stable and somewhat more than conservative. His father, Rabbi Solomon Katz, hailed from a very long line of highly respected rabbis. Nothing less was to be expected from Josh. He was expected to become a rabbi. It was tradition. Anything else would have been unheard of. His future was set in stone.

Ben's mother was a poor working single mom by the

time he was born. His father had abandoned the family months before. There were no expectations placed on him, other than survival. He would have to excel at it. He did. Ben's future was written in sand and changed with each wave that reached it. He took it all in stride, and with each wave simply built another sand castle.

They were an odd pairing to be sure. Ben was good-humored, mischievous, muscular, and husky. Josh was serious, studious, tall, and lean. They were easy to tell apart from each other, but difficult to keep apart from each other. The boys' differences seemed to make them even more drawn to each other. "I guess that opposites attract," Uncle Josh would later say. "You certainly were attractive," Mother would reply.

Mother claims to have been attracted to Josh from the moment their bassinets first touched. "He had me at 'Goo'!" Mother would say. "If they didn't have me strapped in that bassinet, I would have taken him right there."

"It's no wonder I turned out so straight," Uncle Josh would laugh. "I'm pretty sure that they had to move me into an incubator for my own protection."

Though Josh's sexuality may have occasionally come into question due to association, Ben's never was. From the moment he was born everyone knew that Barbie had real competition. He was the boy in flamboyant. That could have been trouble for Ben and his Ken-like best friend if Ben hadn't also been built like GI Joe.

"I was like this walking doll house," Mother, who never met a metaphor he didn't like, would say, "muscled like

Joe, flat-chested like Barbie, great in a fight, better in heels. Unfortunately, I was built more like Barbie's playhouse than any of its skinny little inhabitants."

He may not have been actually as big as a playhouse, but he was certainly a walking powerhouse, and that, added to a tremendous sense of humor, afforded the boys all the protection they would ever need in a fairly tough neighborhood.

"Besides," Mother would add, "I was too big for any of those cute little Barbie outfits that could have gotten me into trouble, so they dressed me up like a lesbian to make me look like all the other boys."

Throughout their early years, the two best friends played together, went to the same public schools, studied together, and often ate together in Josh's home. Ben's home was not kosher, so they only snacked there. On the occasional sleepovers, the boys would build tents and pretend to go camping. "I guess that we had very different ideas about what that meant," Mother would say. "To Joshie it was an adventure; to me it was a career."

With the exception of Josh's Hebrew studies, it was nearly impossible to keep the two boys apart. And even there, when possible, Ben helped Josh with his lessons. When studies were over, Josh would play Mickey Rooney to Ben's Judy Garland and they would put on a play, a drama for Josh, always a musical when it was Ben's turn to choose. They even helped each other with whatever household chores or errands they had. This went on for years until it seemed that nothing could possibly come between them. Then something almost did: Ruthie.

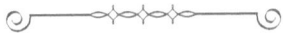

Three

Uncle Josh once told me that "It is God's intent that life begin with an act of love." That may sound a bit idealistic, and the road to hell may actually be paved with good intentions, but I know that Mother and Dad went down a rather difficult road to bring me into their family. And they did so with the best of intentions. They did so because they loved me.

It was Mother who rocked me in his arms and told me made-up funny stories about Aunt Sue and Aunt Allie when I was afraid or sad. It was he who sang me to sleep, drove me to school, took me shopping, and taught me how to go the extra smile when life got me down. And it was he who nursed me when I was sick, nursed me when I was healthy, played with me when I was lonely, and did his best to make everything that was good for me fun.

It was Dad who would take me to the park to play catch, even though neither one of us could really throw or catch a ball. It was he who tried to hit softballs to me, only to watch them drop like flies. And it was Dad who gave me piggy-back rides, helped me with my homework, and encouraged me to be the best at whatever I tried to do.

So, it is with their act of love and their good intentions that my life, my part of the story, begins.

For as early as I can remember, we lived on the Lower Eastside of Manhattan, not far from where Mother and Uncle Josh grew up. In retrospect, our apartment in a tenement building on Avenue A was tiny, but it never felt that way. We were close together, three people in three rooms, but we all seemed to find our space. It is amazing how families have a way of doing that.

The schedules of our extended family balanced well the entire time we lived there. Dad worked weekdays in the Wall Street area, while Mother ran the house and me. On the weekend, Mother worked late nights at the Kit Kat Club where he and the aunts performed. Dad would baby-sit with me on Friday nights, and Uncle Josh would watch me on Saturday nights after the Sabbath so that Dad could catch Mother's performance at the club. On Sunday, everyone would get together at our place for an early dinner, conversation, and playtime. Every day ran perfectly, and every week was strong.

Sometime after my tenth birthday, however, clouds rolled in to darken our perfect daze. A parent's objection to my playing with their child in a parochial school playground because of my "parental situation" led to a huge confrontation in the principal's office. The objection probably would have been dismissed, and the whole incident would have been a non-event, had the objection been raised in a public school. But this was a parochial school, and the clergy have a way of turning non-events into eventful crusades, inquisitions, plagues, and witch-hunts.

Mother, Dad and the other set of parents were called into the principal's office to discuss "the situation." From what I understand, the discussion didn't last long. Mother, with his usual flare for the dramatic, quickly left the school official the victim of his own inquisition. And as for the objecting parents, they were reduced to ashes in the bonfire of their own bigotry, as yet another self-righteous, ill-advised crusade bit the dust.

The crusade may have been over, but "the situation" was about to change our lives, nonetheless. It served to help Mother decide that it was time to leave the small-minded school and the small apartment in the old neighborhood for the more hospitable, greener – and in this case, gayer pastures of suburban New Jersey.

Dad, being Dad, agreed.

I was young, however, and didn't understand the decision to move. I felt that I was somehow to blame for the need to do so. I loved our apartment; I knew that we all did. Teary-eyed, I told Mother how sorry I was to be the cause of his losing his home.

He smiled and hugged me. "Genie, you have to understand that you and your father are my home. This is only my apartment. We'll all be moving together, so we'll be bringing our home with us. We haven't lost it. We're simply moving it to a better place."

I may have been young, but I was old enough to understand what he was saying. No matter where we were, as long as we were together, we would always be home.

That summer, after the school year, we moved. Our new suburban home was three times larger than our New York apartment. It was in a predominantly gay area of New Jersey, with an excellent school district, and just a short distance from New York City by car or train. It still afforded Dad the opportunity to commute to work conveniently, and allowed the aunts and Uncle Josh to visit easily.

It also afforded my parents other opportunities. Mother was growing tired of the late-night performances and wanted to retire. Dad wanted a better investment than renting. And much to my chagrin, it afforded both of them an opportunity to consider giving me something that they felt was missing from my life: siblings.

I have to admit that siblings were not something I ever longed for. The visions of sugar plums dancing in their heads was their dream. And I was pretty sure that it would be my nightmare. Being an only child in an extended family has a lot of advantages, and I wasn't sure that I was ready to lose or share them.

Their concern for my concerns bought us all some time. But they were eventually able to convince me of the math, that addition didn't equal subtraction. And they did it by multiplying the addition by two – two of the neediest, most intriguing characters they could possibly find: the twins Chip and Dale.

I did not meet Chip and Dale (Yes, those are their real

names!) until shortly before they were adopted and came to live with us. But I was certainly told a lot about them before time.

Chip is Dale's not so identical twin brother. Dale is his more masculine sister. Chip was taller and had a rather gothic look about him that did not deter from his good looks. Dale was also attractive, rather hefty, strong, and liked to dress like a lumberjack, or rather, a lumber Jill. They were a year younger than me, but they had been forced by difficult circumstances to mature quickly. So, it was not so surprising that, as young as they were, they had already identified their fashion and sexual identities.

Their young lives had always been rather difficult. Their mother died in childbirth. They were raised by an alcoholic father who not only blamed them for her death, but in his drunken hazes would make them pay for whatever pleasures he thought they had deprived him of.

It seems that on a particularly bad night, their father died after falling down a set of stairs with a mysterious bump on his head. It appeared that the bump might have matched one of Chip's wooden clogs, which he wore all the time. The twins weren't talking, but in light of neighbors' testimony and other documentation it was determined to be "an unavoidable accident." After their father's death they had difficulty getting either fostered or adopted into suitable families.

Their counselors at Child Services said they just needed to find the right home where all parties could be comfortable. Voila!

Just to be sure, however, I hung an "Already Disturbed" sign outside my bedroom door. A pound of cure is worth the ounce of prevention.

Life is full of surprises. Mine is never without them. On the day that the twins were supposed to arrive, a technicality held up the adoption paperwork. It would take another week to straighten things out.

Mother and Dad did not come home empty-handed, however. It seems that Uncle Josh had spoken to them about a young man who needed a place to stay until a permanent home could be found for him. They met by chance in a bus station in the city as the boy was arriving from out west somewhere and Uncle Josh was heading to our place in New Jersey. Upon hearing the boy's story, he found himself impressed with the youth's genuineness and honesty. Since he lived in a small studio apartment, he thought our home might be a better temporary solution. He called my parents and asked if they could help. It was Josh. That was enough of an answer. The boy had a place to stay.

Mother entered our home first and attempted to explain the situation. This boy that Uncle Josh met was coming to stay with us for a while. It would only be temporary, a few weeks at most. "He's a nice boy, you'll like him, he's very personable, a real charmer, but because the twins will be here next week, he'll probably have to share your room until we can figure something else out.

I know that this is a lot to take in right now, but you understand. Right, Genie? It's just for a little while."

I have to admit that I was spoiled and didn't understand. I was incensed. This really was too much. My parents were too much. I was just about to throw a major tantrum when Robbie entered the room. My jaw dropped. He was the most beautiful human being that I had ever seen in my short life. He looked something like a young Greek god in farmers' clothes. He could have stepped off the front page of a tractor catalog.

Robbie was fourteen, nearly two years older than me and light years beyond anyone I had ever seen. I didn't move. I couldn't take my eyes off of him. I just stared, dumbfounded. After a few seconds Mother closed my mouth, lifted my hand, and said, "Genie says, 'Hi Robbie! Pleased to meet you.'"

Robbie smiled and his eyes seemed to glisten as he walked across the room. He shook my hand, breezed his fingers through my hair as my jaw dropped open again, and said, "Hi Hot Stuff! I've heard a lot about you. I hope you don't mind my staying for a little while. I'll try not to get in your way."

I think I nodded my head that it was OK. "Great!" he said as his smile grew wider, "How about showing me to our room so I can freshen up a bit? It's been awhile since I've had the opportunity."

Mother stepped behind me and lifted my jaw again saying, "Muscle spasm … it happens sometimes. Genie says, 'follow me,' or him, or whatever."

As I rather awkwardly led Robbie to our room after a little shove from Mother, I heard him say to Dad in the background, "Well, I think that answers a few nagging questions. Don't you?"

I don't know if I even spoke that much to Robbie as he introduced himself to me in our room that first day. I think I just stared at him with some huge grin and listened to every word he said.

He told me his life story. How he was part Lakota and Irish on his father's side and half Swedish on his mother's. How his father died during what should have been a routine operation before Robbie was born. How his Mom remarried, more for his sake than her own, and how abusive his stepfather was to both of them.

He told me how he lived on a farm, how his Mom died while he was still little, and how things got much worse after that. He said that he was often beaten, given little as far as food and clothing, and made to work long hours.

And finally he told me how he was forced to flee for his life after his stepfather had caught him in the barn having sex with an older boy. They grabbed their clothes and ran from the farm. His stepfather ran for his gun and fired shots at them as they escaped through a cornfield with bullets flying past them.

They ran a few miles before they even dared to stop and get dressed. Robbie only had time to grab a shirt and his pants before taking off, so he had to walk the rest of the way into town barefoot. When they got to the older boy's home, they realized that Robbie could never go home again, so the boy gave Robbie some money, clothes and shoes, and put him on a bus to New York.

I could hear the trauma creeping into Robbie's voice as he explained how he was so confused and didn't know where to turn when he arrived in New York. People in the bus terminal were rushing everywhere. There were so many people, yet no one to talk to. Then again he didn't know what to say or what to ask. He knew nothing about New York and had no idea what to do or where to go after he left the terminal. He felt so hopeless, so lost.

And then, just as he felt the tears running down his cheek and despair starting to cripple him, he felt a strong hand on his shoulder. He did not know him, but he immediately sensed that this man was a kind, good man. And so, with nothing to lose, he told this man his story, the whole story. And now, thanks to that gentle rabbi, here he was in our home, for the first time in a long time, safe, home.

I heard the whole story. I hung on every word. It all registered. I wanted to say something comforting, to hug him. I wanted to make him feel at home. But my thoughts froze in a replay loop of the sex part, and my body apparently followed suit. I didn't move. I didn't say a word. I put the dumb in dumbfounded.

Later that night, just before dinner, I showered and changed while Robbie unpacked his few belongings. Shortly afterward I arrived at the dinner table to a rather surprised reaction from Mother and Dad. "What?" I asked as their eyes lit up the huge grins below.

"Nothing!" they said in unison. "We were just admiring the usual sprucing-up for dinner," Mother grinned further. "Nothing at all, really."

The dinner conversation was mostly small talk about our room, the house, making yourself at home, etc. Mother and Dad already knew most of Robbie's story and saw no need to rehash anything. Through most of the dinner I sat quietly trying to think of something impressive to say. I was at a loss. I had to settle for the more Zen approach, silence of the lamas.

The one time that I did try to be a little clever, however, I managed to poke my cheek with my fork while trying to eat and joke at the same time. I drew blood and Mother's immediate medical attention. "Enough with the pockmarks," Mother joked, "You're too young for the Brad Pitt look." Needless to say, I wasn't extremely impressive.

Later while we were doing the dishes, I confessed to Robbie that I was a little nervous and that I just wanted him to like me. He smiled and said, "Hot Stuff, you have no idea how nervous I am right now. I'm trying to do my best to fit in. I want you to like me, too. I want you all to like me. I guess that we all have a little adjusting to do. But don't worry, you're doing just fine. I'm more comfortable with you than I have been around anyone in a long time, maybe ever."

That night, when Robbie and I retired to our room, I was more excited than I had ever been in my life. As we talked, Robbie slowly started to undress. I could hardly follow the conversation. I felt a bit like some sleazy voyeur, but I couldn't help myself. I was so flushed with excitement that I could hardly speak. I mumbled enough to keep the conversation going until he was completely undressed and had climbed into the spare bed that my parents set up. It was the first live naked body that I had ever seen, or, at least the first one that I had ever paid attention to.

I asked him if he needed pajamas or anything and was relieved when he said that he was more comfortable sleeping without anything on. He asked if I was comfortable with his being naked, and I had to hold back on the enthusiasm of my yes, while trying to inconspicuously adjust the part of me that suddenly wasn't so comfortable.

If Robbie sensed the emotional tornado swirling inside me, he kept it to himself. After a few more pleasantries, he turned off the light next to his bed, said, "Good night, Hot Stuff!" pulled a sheet over his naked body, and quickly fell asleep.

That night, I watched the impression of his body under the sheet, watched as his curly blond hair and striking facial features faded into the dark night, studied the shape and length of his foot as it dangled over the side of the bed, occasionally twitching to dreams I longed to see and be a part of.

All night long I felt the tornado swirling, lifting, pulling inside me. These were feelings that I had never felt before. And I knew one thing for certain. They felt right, they were exciting, and I never wanted them to end.

Robbie's barn story and the images of him that night became a newsreel that I would often play over and over again in my mind.

The next morning, I watched Robbie wake up and climb out of bed. My mind was still filming. He must have sensed that I was awake all night. He sat down on my bed, still naked from the night before. He smiled almost knowingly and running his fingers through my hair as he did the day before, said with a wink, "Hey, Hot Stuff, you look pretty tired. You didn't stay awake all night and take advantage of me while I slept, did you?"

I could feel my face turn crimson. I tried to say something, but choked. I was afraid that I had been discovered, that he could read my mind. I was afraid that he somehow sensed how much I wanted just to touch him.

Sensing my embarrassment, he quickly apologized. "Just kidding, Buddy, really. I was only teasing you. I'm sorry! I never meant to embarrass you. It was a dumb joke. I didn't mean anything by it. I was just playing because I want us to be friends. You're kind of like the little brother I've always wanted, so I was trying to be funny. You're such a good kid, I know you wouldn't do anything like that. I'm really sorry if I embarrassed you. Forgive me?"

"Yeah! Of course!" I gulped as my fears and my crimson began to fade, "It's OK!" Which, of course it was. Anything that Robbie did at that point would have been OK. "I'm really glad you're here."

"Me too, little brother!" he said, as I once again watched in awe while he stood up and walked naked into the shower, and into every naked fiber of my being. "Me too."

Later that morning, as my voice returned, and I was actually able to carry on a decent conversation, I filled Robbie in on everything he needed to know about the family. I told him everything I knew about Mother and Dad and our lives together. I told him all that I knew about Uncle Josh. I told him about Aunt Allie and Aunt Sue, both of whom he would soon meet, and about the twins who would soon be living with us. I told him everything I could think of to keep his time and attention focused on me, on us.

I remember how he smiled and his eyes twinkled at my stories; and how we laughed and joked about Chip and Dale's names. He laughed even more when I told him how my last name was Poole-Hall, Poole like Mother's and my mom's, and Hall like Dad's.

"Your family sounds so wonderful," he said almost sadly. "I hope that I'll have enough time to get to know them all, but I don't know how long I'll be staying here."

"Forever!" I said with all my heart. "You have to stay forever!"

I suppose that nobody stays anywhere forever. One thing was for sure. However long Robbie was going to be staying with us, it wasn't going to be with just the clothes on his back and the few changes he brought with him, not if Mother could help it, and there is never a time when Mother can't help it.

He packed us all into Dad's car, took us to the mall, and despite Robbie's protests that my parents had already done too much for him, he returned later in the day with a wardrobe any teenager would be proud of. Mother was phenomenal, he lives for such days. He transposed Robbie off the cover of Modern Farmer onto the cover of

Modern Teen. I don't think I've ever seen so many tears of happiness in my life. Robbie cried some, too.

The whole Robbie whirlwind was so exciting that by the time the twins arrived a week later it was almost a non-event. Robbie and I were already inseparable, and although I tried to be friendly and polite to the newcomers, Robbie remained the focus of most of my attention, even at the twins' Welcome Home party.

Robbie was far more welcoming than I, however, and did his best to make the twins feel as at home as we had tried to make him feel. He even helped them pick out wardrobes to fit their individual tastes on Mother's next day shopping extravaganza. His good looks and charm quickly won them over, and I did my best to ride shotgun and just go along for the ride.

It was the beginning of summer, and Mother and Dad were ecstatic over their new brood. Apparently, they had always talked about having a large family; now, in less than a month's time, here it was, a full house. Mother quit performing at the club to become a full-time parent, something he had planned to do for some time anyway Aunt Sue and Aunt Allie decided that it just wasn't the same without him and soon followed suit. Dad continued to work at his Wall Street job to meet the new financial demands. And the weekend visits of the aunts and Uncle Josh recommenced once everything had settled down.

The first visit with the aunts was quite the experience for Robbie, Chip and Dale. They had never experienced drag performers before, and the aunts, knowing this, arrived in full regalia. Mother later remarked that he thought that we were being invaded by gay piñatas, ready to explode chintz and sequins all over the place.

"It's show time, everybody!" shouted Aunt Sue clapping his hands as they burst through our front door. "Stations and places, everybody! The show must go on. And quick, lots of makeup for Mother; there's no time to lose."

"This is the most adorable audience I've ever seen," Aunt Allie added. "Let the festivities begin." And, of course they did. The aunts even convinced Mother to dress up for the occasion, something I had never seen. Within the hour the entire downstairs of our house had been transported to a burlesque hall where Mother and the aunts joked, sang, danced, and did impersonations of old people that we had never heard of, but that were still funny. For the hours that followed, they filled the house with more love and warmth than anyone could possibly imagine, and then some. It was the first of hundreds of such magical nights.

When your life is bigger than life, the show always goes on.

Uncle Josh had missed all the festivities that first night because of the Sabbath, but when he arrived that Saturday night it started all over again. The show went on, sans Mother who was busy cooking and serving this time.

After all the getting to know each other, eating, and activities had finished, Uncle Josh retired with Robbie and me to our room, and the aunts went with Chip and Dale to their room to set up additional "camp" grounds and play games, while Mother and Dad finished cleaning up.

NORMAL?

It was a ritual that we would repeat often. All of us loved it, and the pairings worked perfectly. Though, to my thinking, Robbie and I got the better of the deal.

Uncle Josh, Robbie, and I didn't play games in our room. Instead, Uncle Josh would tell us stories, usually about some part of the extended family. He was a wonderful story teller, and the first story he told Robbie and me was about how Mother and Dad first met.

Four

"First," he began, "let me tell you about the kind of person your Uncle Benji was." He never stopped calling Mother by his childhood name. "Even when he was little, which was practically never, Benji was like this big superhero that always made everyone feel safe. He never allowed anyone to pick on anyone else. He was Supermensch. If you were in trouble, in a flash he was there. And believe me, he made sure the troublemakers never bothered you again.

On one such occasion, I remember there was this little boy, a few years younger than us, maybe about six, who was taking a beating from three boys a few years older than us, about ten. We were in a different neighborhood, so Benji and I didn't know any of the boys. But that didn't stop him, nothing could. He was always the shining knight that saved the day.

Before anyone knew what happened, all three of the bullies were on the ground with their heads smashed together like a big pretzel between Benji's enormous hands.

And there was Benji, warning them that if they ever so much as looked at that little boy the wrong way again, they would be in the ground, not on it.

When he was sure that they had learned their lesson, he let them up, made them apologize, and chased them away. Then he helped the little boy off the ground, dusted him off, wiped the tears from his eyes, and told him that if he ever needed help again he'd be there. Which, of course he would have been. That's the kind of person your Uncle Benji was, or rather is.

He didn't see that little boy again, so we'll fast forward fourteen or fifteen years to 'Minnie Van,' aka Mother, aka, Benji, performing at the Kit Kat Club. Benji, as you can imagine, was the star of the show at this point. Most nights the show was sold out.

Over the course of a couple of performances this one particular month, Benji began to notice this nice young man sitting by himself in the corner. Night after night he would watch Benji perform and then disappear, only to re appear again the following week and repeat the cycle. This was particularly odd since most of the show's performances were basically the same, so one or two viewings should be more than enough for anyone, believe me.

On one very different night, however, the young man again showed up, this time with two bouquets of flowers, which did not escape Benji's attention. And after Benji finished performing, he walked over to the young man's table and asked, 'Are the flowers for me, or are you just trying to class the place up?'

The young man responded, 'This one's for you.' as he handed Benji one of the bouquets.

'And the other?' Benji asked.

'The other is for the person I'm hoping to ask out after the performance,' said the young man rather shyly.

'And who might that be, if you don't mind me asking?' Benji asked, not really caring whether the young man minded or not.

To which the young admirer replied, 'They're for that person you become when you take off your costumes and makeup, and then quietly step out the back door after each show.'

Benji at first was both taken aback and flattered, but he'd been down that road before with guys caught up by the persona in the show. And so he responded 'Oh, Honey! You don't really know that person. You know the costumes and glitter that can be anyone you want them to be, but you don't know that other person.'

And the young man smiled and said, 'I've searched for that person longer than you can imagine. I know him better than you think. He saved me from being beaten by three young thugs when I was a little boy. My family moved away soon after that and I never saw him again.

After he walked out of my life on the day that he rescued me, I swore that someday I would find him, and I wouldn't let him walk out of my life again. And now, here we are. So how about it? Do the damn flowers get me a date?'

And the rest, as they say, is history."

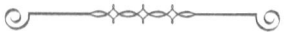

Five

I went to bed that night understanding more about my parents than I ever did before. And I loved them even more because of it. I started to replay their meeting in my head. It played so romantic. Then Robbie started to get undressed for bed. My mind had to choose between visions of my parents' romance or Robbie having sex in the barn. I couldn't help it. I was a kid, and Robbie was the closest I'd ever been to sex anywhere.

The next day, which was Sunday, was about to become another family tradition. Uncle Josh and the aunts had stayed over, and it was decided that we were going to have a large family dinner. Mother asked Uncle Josh and the aunts to take us somewhere for the afternoon so that he and Dad would have time to prepare. We chose a nearby science museum.

The museum was great. We were all having fun and either seriously discussing or joking about the various exhibits until we got to the exhibit on insects. Aunts Allie and

Sue were going on and on about how beautiful all the butterflies in the glass cases were, but Uncle Josh looked rather sad. When I asked what was bothering him, he said that he didn't want to be a killjoy, but they were beautiful, not are.

"It was their life that made them beautiful," he said sadly. "The colorful remains from their death cannot compare to the majesty that was taken from them. I am sure that like all creatures, they wanted to live, that they each had a purpose. And I'm sure that they felt pain.

Imagine if we took all the beautiful people and all the beautiful creatures that we love and pinned them lifeless inside some glass cases just to admire them. Not so beautiful! It may be educational. It may seem important. But, it is not so beautiful. Maybe I'm getting too sentimental as I get older, but as I look at them, I feel their loss far more than I see my gain."

On the way home, I kept thinking about what Uncle Josh said and how sad it made him. I kept picturing the dead butterflies, wondering what they would look like if they were still alive and able to move their wings. All through Mother's dinner, I wanted to tell Uncle Josh that I understood and believed in what he was saying, but at the same time I didn't want to offend the aunts who were still gushing over the beauty of the dead butterflies. So I waited until after dinner, and asked to be excused. I went to my room and wrote him this story, hoping that he would get the message without offending anyone else.

Six

THE LESSON

By Gene Poole-Hall

(Age 12)

Curiosity among the bison was unherd of. It was as big a danger to the entire herd as it was to the individual. There were many predators both within and without their protected area. Curiosity brought attention. Attention was seldom a good thing.

The first lesson that Biff's mother taught him when he was a young calf was that he must always stay within the confines of their herd, and within limits of the park preserve where they lived. The size of the bison herd was rather formidable, and so it offered the young calf much protection if he just abided by the rules.

Outside the preserve, however, Biff was told that there was extreme danger, and there were no rules. The predators there were much fiercer, and the size of the herd mattered little. These predators had forgotten the natural order of things, and adopted savage practices that the other creatures did not understand. They seldom hunted for only what they needed to survive, and actually seemed to enjoy killing just for the sake taking another creature's life. Sometimes they would do very strange things and take only the heads of their victims, or sometimes just their horns and antlers. Stranger still, sometimes they would take nothing at all except their victim's life. It was a practice no other creature would ever understand.

The elders in the herd told Biff and the other young calves legends of a very different relationship with these predators. The legends were from generations ago when all creatures roamed free, and when the predators' skin was much darker. It was a time when these creatures also understood and lived according to the natural order.

Back then, the predators understood that all creatures want to live a natural life, that they all experience fear, and they all feel pain. The old predators were wiser then. They hunted only for what they needed to survive. They demonstrated respect for the lives of all their fellow creatures. And it is said that they offered both thanks and regret to the Creator of All Things and to their victim's spirit when they were forced to take a life.

Those times are long gone, the calves were told. The dark-skinned creatures seemed to have disappeared, and the lighter-skinned species that replaced them often do not appear to understand any natural order at all. They have little or no respect for their fellow creatures. There is no regret or thanks expressed to the Creator or their victims. They treat all life as though it was meant solely for their pleasure. It is even said that rather than hunt, they herd some creatures into tiny horrible spaces, force horrible feed into them to make them bigger, and then, when they are fatted, take their lives without respect – in fear and in pain.

As horrible as that may sound, it is not the worst. That treatment is only for the creatures that sustain them. Many of their other victims have been killed off completely for no reason whatsoever. You can no longer find them in the wild, but you can find parts of them still hanging in places where these hunters live.

We are much larger than them, but we are not immune. Once we were among the most numerous creatures on earth. You could not count our numbers. You could not measure our home. Then these creatures came. Now you can count us. Now you can measure.

The elders told these things to the young calves not to frighten them, but to warn them that there was true danger outside of their protected area. None of the bison knew for certain why the light-skinned creatures seldom hunted in the preserve, but they knew that those of their number that ventured outside its protection never returned.

These stories were enough to scare most of the calves into following the herd's rules on boundaries, which was a good thing. Unfortunately the stories were also enough to pique curiosity in Biff and two of his friends. For young bison, this was seldom a good thing.

Stephen J. Mulrooney

Biff and his friends, Scruff and Fuzz, were determined to see what these light-skinned creatures really looked like. It seemed impossible that any creature could be that ferocious, that ignorant of the natural order of things. All creatures exhibit some form of order, some form of intelligence, they reasoned. Surely these creatures must have some. They had to find out for themselves.

One night while the herd was resting, the three friends slipped into the woods surrounding the plains where they lived. They seldom ventured into the woods, so they were not sure exactly where they were going. They were confident, however, that if they were patient enough, eventually they would spy one of the creatures that they sought. They had to see for themselves if such creatures really existed.

They walked along a stream where they knew there were beavers. They had often seen beavers before, but not like these. These beavers were different. These beavers did not move. They were bloodied and no longer had life in them. They had not been eaten as one would expect from a predator. They apparently were not killed for food, nor protection, nor for any apparent reason whatsoever; so they knew that this must be the work of the light-skinned ones. The young bison were afraid. Scruff and Fuzz talked of turning back, but at Biff's insistence they moved on.

A little further into the woods, Biff and his friends found a few squirrels and an opossum in similar condition to the beavers. How confusing, they thought, different creatures, still no apparent reason. Why would they possibly be left like this? Still farther there were a few

44

more squirrels and three birds, all bloodied and without life. What type of creature would do such a thing, they wondered, and why?

Their fear had grown enough. Once again, they heard the warnings of their parents and their elders in their heads. They now understood that they were in real danger. They were about to turn back when they heard strange noises from just outside the woods. Curiosity got the best of fear, and Biff, Scruff, and Fuzz inched further, hoping to see without being seen.

There they were, the light-skinned creatures, and they were surrounded by deer and elk in the same condition as the smaller creatures along their path, all without life. The light-skinned creatures were making loud noises, and drinking out of strangely shaped things and then breaking them on the rocks. There was the blood of other creatures all around, and the light-skinned ones were throwing their victims on top of large strangely shaped things and tying them there. There was no reverence for what they were doing, or had done, no thanks, no respect. The bison knew that the Creator of All Things could not be happy with these creatures.

The young bison had seen more than enough. They understood the real danger. They tried to slip away as quietly as possible, but the woods' floor is not silent. Their steps alerted the hunters. The hunters picked up strange sticks and started after them. Their sticks made strange noises and the other branches and trees around them started to explode. The young bison ran as fast as they could. Biff felt something whiz by him that sounded like a bee, but scarier. It exploded into a tree. Then the noises stopped.

Biff continued to run. He felt that he had escaped, but he could not take the chance. He would not stop. He would not feel safe until they were back with the herd. Then it hit him. He was alone. The young bison had all scattered when the noise started exploding things and must have gone in separate directions. Biff was terrified. Where were his friends? Were they safe? Did the noises stop because they too were now without life?

Biff had never experienced such panic before, and he felt hopeless and ashamed. He and his friends had failed to heed the most important lesson they were given, and may have paid the ultimate price for it. He decided to go and confess to the elders what they had done, and hope that they could help in some way to find out what happened to his friends.

When Biff reached the Bison plain, he could sense that the herd had already been looking for the missing calves. How could he possibly explain this terrible thing that may have happened to Scruff and Fuzz? How could their parents ever forgive him? How could he ever forgive himself?

As he stepped out of the woods, something amazing took place. At the far end of the woods, Scruff and Fuzz stepped out at the same time. They ran to each other and butted heads to show how happy they were to be back together. They butted and danced their way back to the herd. They knew that they were in trouble, but that was OK.

They were alive and had learned a valuable lesson. After accepting the scolding that they knew they deserved, and expressing their apologies, they vowed their future obedience to the rules of the herd.

That night the elders took the calves aside and asked them to relate all that they had seen. Biff and his friends told their story as faithfully as they could remember. When they had finished and were dismissed to return to their parents, Biff lagged behind to speak to the lead bull of the herd.

The lead bull was not only the strongest of the herd, but the wisest. Biff asked him if he thought that there was any hope for the herd while such creatures as these hunters existed. The lead bull nodded that there is always hope, but that their hope also rests with these light-skinned creatures. "There is far more good in them than bad," he said. "We have only warned you about the bad in them because it is not always easy to distinguish who is good among them. So for our safety, we try to avoid them all.

But understand this: It is the good in them that protects us on these plains. As the natural order has learned to live with them, so too are they once again learning to live with it. We are all of One Creator, but the survival of all more and more appears to depend on them.

Like us, like all creatures, they too want to live; they too know fear; they too feel pain. They are just like us, yet different. We can only hope that the best of them brings out the best in them."

Seven

Later that night, when it was just the two of us, I gave my story to Uncle Josh. "I've never written anything like this," I prefaced as I handed it to him, "but I hope that it gets my point across. I just wanted to let you know that I believe in everything you were saying this afternoon."

Uncle Josh put on his reading glasses and sat down on my bed near the desk lamp. Before he began to read he said, "You know that this is already the best story I have ever read." I smiled and he said, "You may think that I'm kidding, but I already feel your heart in the story, so it has already touched mine."

After he finished reading it, he put down his glasses, smiled and said, "You know, I really am smarter than I thought. This really is the best story I've ever read."

"You don't have to say that," I said. "I just wanted to find a way to tell you how I felt. I chose this way because I think that I may want to be a writer some day."

"Too late, my son," he replied with a huge smile, "you already are."

When we rejoined the rest of the family, Uncle Josh asked if he could share the gift I had given him with everyone else. "You are too talented to be embarrassed," he chided. "I predict that a great career begins here."

So, at his urging, I read my story. And when I was done, Mother and the aunts showered me with happy tears. Dad gave me a huge hug and the twins high-fived me. Robbie threw his arms around me, kissed the top of my head and told me that he couldn't be more proud of me if I actually was his little brother. Damn! I thought. I really do want to be a writer!

The rest of the evening, the thought of becoming a writer swam in my head. Fiction I thought, I would love to be a fiction writer. I spend most of my time in the realm of imagination anyway, so why not write about what I know. Facts confuse so many people, but fiction is supposed to. That makes fiction a more realistic, less confusing choice.

"Why not just write about whatever you're feeling at the time?" Robbie asked later when I told him my idea, "The rest will just come naturally." But, as we spoke, and I watched Robbie undress and slip under the top sheet that perfectly silhouetted his form, I decided that writing about what I felt at the time may not be such a good idea. I worried about what else might come naturally. I decided that I had better stick to fiction.

Eight

Robbie, Chip, Dale and I spent a lot of time during the following weeks getting to know each other better. I was becoming more and more fond of the twins, though I somewhat resented sharing so much of my time with Robbie. All of our attention seemed to revolve around him, and I could tell that Chip and Dale looked up to him as much as I did. We followed him everywhere, like chicks in his brood. And the amazing part was that he really seemed to enjoy our company, and sought us out as much as we did him.

The Friday night of our fifth week together was somewhat quieter than expected with my parents and the aunts spending most of the time in a private conversation that excluded the rest of us. None of us knew what the secrecy was about, and the seriousness of the grown ups demeanor wasn't giving anything away. In this family that felt foreboding.

The next evening, Saturday night, after Uncle Josh arrived, we finally learned what the secrecy was all about. Dad broke the news at dinner. "Uncle Josh and I have been working pretty hard this past month trying to straighten out Robbie's living situation. It was difficult because it involved legalities in multiple states, finding the right family willing to take him in, and figuring out his schooling situation."

I could feel the color drain from all the youngest faces in the room, probably mine as much as Robbie's. "Fortunately," Dad continued, "the process did not have to include Robbie's stepfather who apparently never had nor filed for any type of legal guardianship, and who can't seem to be located anyway. That could have been a huge complication for his new family."

I could barely see out of the tears welling in my eyes, but I knew that Robbie, Chip's and Dale's eyes were no drier.

"So!" Dad continued. "We all hope that Robbie will be happy with what we came up with. Robbie, if you'll have us, we would love for you to become a permanent member of our little circus." And then looking at Chip, Dale and me, "Am I right, you clowns?"

The dams burst and the tears gushed forth from all our eyes. We all ran around hugging, and kissing, and soaking each other. Then, without even need of an answer from Robbie, Mother brought out a "Welcome Home 4 Ever Robbie" cake with lit candles and sparklers all over it.

"Make a wish," Mother said as he placed the cake in front of Robbie.

"No need!" Robbie replied through his tears. "It's already come true."

That night, without a doubt, we had the best party we ever had.

Later, when my new brother and I retired with Uncle Josh for story time, Robbie had the honor of choosing the topic. He asked to learn more about the aunts.

"That's a tough request," Uncle Josh said with a grin. I promised myself not to tell tales about Sue and Allie any more. Fortunately, however, I didn't promise to tell them any less."

Nine

"Sue is a tough one," Uncle Josh began. "You probably know as much about him as I do. Not even Benji knows the history of this mysterious character. By the time that your uncle came to work at the Kit Kat Club, Sue's name had been legally changed to his stage name. If you asked Sue anything about the past, all he would say was that he was in the Jehovah Witness Protection Program and couldn't discuss it. As far as I know, he never discussed his past with anyone. And if his boyfriend knew anything about it, he never mentioned it.

You both look surprised. Yes! When your uncle introduced me to Sue, he had a boyfriend, a somewhat unsavory character. I'll call him Big Al, because that was his name. Big Al had what you might call connections, so if you wanted to keep all the ones in your body, you didn't cross him.

Since your uncle hadn't met Tom, your Dad, yet, I would go and watch the show to give Benji support. Much to my chagrin, Big Al, after our initial introduction, began to sit at my table. It was a forgettable experience that I will never forget. Anything that he repeated about Sue should never have been repeated. It had much more to do with sexual innuendos and acrobatics than history. It was the type of talk that would tattoo images in your brain that a lobotomy couldn't remove.

Fortunately for everybody, including me, Sue got involved in the Stonewall Riots soon after that. Big Al, not willing to risk any sort of exposure, quickly ended his relationship with Sue and, thankfully, with me. It was as if I had passed a mental kidney stone.

As far as I know, Sue never saw Big Al again, nor anyone else for that matter. He often says that, 'Mother got me over the hump of Big Al, and I've never been humped again.' And you'll have to forgive me for repeating that but some of Sue's sayings are like bad sausages. They just repeat themselves.

After that, the rest of Sue is as much a mystery to me as it is to you. The only real social connection I have ever really had with him is through Benji and your Dad. We did run into each other once a few years back at a mutual friend's party. He was on the way out as I arrived. 'Don't even bother to go in,' he warned me as he passed by. 'All they have is crackers and dips, and that's just the guest list.' I thought it was rather rude, but as it turned out, it was rather observant.

In conclusion, I will tell you this though. You couldn't have a fiercer friend, or a fiercer foe. And, as for you children, you couldn't possibly have a better guardian angel, even if he does seem to be more Hell's than Heaven's sometimes."

"Ali, on the other hand," Uncle Josh continued, "is another story, lots of chapters, some also mysterious. First of all, you probably didn't even know that he has a twin, an identical twin, Mohammed. Identical is almost a misnomer in this case because, except for looks, each twin is what the other is not. Mohammed is a strong tough guy; Ali is not. Mohammed works for the police department; Ali, because times were different and his manner of dress was not always legally acceptable, has probably spent more time there than Mohammed. Mohammed is an expert in martial arts, Ali in fine arts. Mohammed looks like one of the boys; Ali likes to look at the boys. They're both single and live together, but they are never seen together. It's almost as though they were one person with two very distinct personalities.

Their history is very interesting. And I'm not sure how much of it I'm at liberty to discuss. So I'll tell it all. It begins in Iran, just before the Islamic Revolution.

Ali and Mohammed's father was a pretty well-known alcoholic with an extremely bad temper when he drank, which was all the time. When he wasn't beating his wife over some ridiculous provocation, he would beat Ali, but never Mohammed whom he favored for some reason. Even when Mohammed tried to prevent his mother and brother from being beaten, Ali would get the worst of it.

Ali's way of dealing with the drinking and beatings was

to escape into fantasy. He would pretend that he was famous movie stars, or singers, mostly women, and would
put on shows for his mother and brother, who loved them.
This of course, all took place while Ali's father was not
home.

Ali would create costumes out of his mother's clothing and scarves. He would design background sets out of
sheets and other materials. And he would use household
spices for makeup. The costumes and sets and makeup
grew more and more elaborate as he got older, all without
his father's knowledge.

I think that you can guess that this was not going to last
forever. One day, when the boys were about ten or eleven,
their father came home raging drunk in the middle of the
afternoon, and in the middle of one of Ali's performances.
Everything hit the wall, especially Ali, who was taking a
terrible beating.

When Mohammed tried to intervene, his father
knocked the wind out of him and locked him in a closet.
When their mother tried to help her son, the poor woman
was knocked unconscious. After beating his son some
more, this wretched man grabbed Ali, saying that if he
wanted to be treated like a woman, he would treat him like
one. He dragged Ali into the bedroom and started to put
him through an unconscionable horror that he probably
would not have survived. And even if he did, no victim of
this type of abuse ever completely survives.

Fortunately, Ali's screaming and crying were more
than Mohammed, who truly loved his brother, could take.

Mohammed burst out of the closet, picked up the nearest thing he could find, which was a lamp, and put an end to the horror forever.

Remember, by now the Islamic Revolution had come to Iran. These were difficult times for anyone or anything different. The boys' mother was afraid that the only one who would appear innocent in the whole scenario under the new regime was the dead, abusive husband and father. So she had Ali quickly pack traveling bags for them all while she and Mohammed buried her husband in their back yard. She then took the boys to her parents' home, saying nothing except that they were escaping another night of her husband's abuse.

The next day, without even her parents' knowledge, she quickly arranged for the three of them to ostensibly visit her gravely ill sister in Cairo, who was neither gravely ill nor lived in Cairo. From there they made it to New York, where they sought and were granted asylum. The poor woman passed away a few years after that from a heart condition, and the two boys have been together ever since, inseparable in their separate lives."

Uncle Josh got up to leave and join the others. "Next time," he said, "I'll tell you about how Benji saved Ali's career."

That was too much to leave hanging for Robbie and me, and we begged him mercilessly to continue. So, he sat back down and started, "Well, I'm not one to tell stories, but …

Soon after Benji joined the Kit Kat Club, it was decided by management that they were going to build a new, younger show around him. Sue's job was safe because of Big Al's connections. Kaye, whom you children wouldn't really know, was young enough to survive. But Ali, or should I say Allie Kat since we're talking show biz, had been with the club a long time with no real change in his act to speak of. Nor were his impersonations the best, which didn't help, I might add.

Now, it seems that the stage manager had a young boyfriend that nobody but he liked. However, the young man could do all of Allie's impersonations, only better. When the manager tried to replace Allie with him, everyone objected, but the manager insisted that the boy had talent on his side. Benji, already known as Mother to them, suggested a competition in front of a live audience, with the winner getting the job. The manager readily agreed, knowing the boy's talent, and was further thrilled when Benji suggested 'Dueling Dietrichs.' Marlene Dietrich was the specialty of his young friend.

On the night of the performance, Allie was a wreck. He kept throwing salt over his shoulder and kissing a rabbit's foot. Benji warned him that it was bad luck to be superstitious, but that didn't stop him. If Benji hadn't been there with him, he probably would never have gone on. It looked bleak.

The rest of the crew was already starting to say their goodbyes. Benji took Allie aside and made him put on a special corset that he made for his 'Falling in Love Again' number. Benji then slapped a face on him that looked way too clownish for the seriousness that Allie always brought to the number. Allie knew he had nothing to lose, so he promised to do everything that Benji asked him to do, including not stopping the song no matter what happened on stage.

Gale went first. That was the young friend's stage name, Gale Wind, or Gale Storm, or some other name that blows, if you'll excuse the pun.

Anyway, Gale went first and was dynamic to say the least. He got a great reception. All looked lost. Sue, Kaye, and Benji came out and sat at my table to watch. Everyone but Benji was worried.

When Allie entered, his over-the-top appearance drew a laugh. This disturbed him enough that he inadvertently made a frightened face that made him look even funnier. As he started to sing, he sat with the chair facing backwards, the way Dietrich would.

Then it happened. The corset felt uncomfortable and started to stick on the chair. He tried to get up, but the chair got up with him, and stuck between his legs. Still singing, he pushed and pulled and yanked at the chair, all to no avail. It was almost like it was glued between his legs. The more he struggled to remove it while he sang, the funnier his expressions became and the more the audience laughed.

The heavy-duty Velcro material that Benji sewed on the corset and on the chair was so strong that Allie started tripping and staggering all around the stage trying to dislodge the chair, but never stopping the song. It was hysterical; the audience was in an uproar. By the time he hobbled off the stage, chair in tow, the audience was rolling. He got a standing ovation, a job, and a new act all in one shot. And all due to the creative genius of 'you know who.'"

Uncle Josh got up after finishing his story, patted us both on the head, and said, "Now let's not go around repeating how Mohammed accidentally killed his father. It would probably upset Ali, and it's not always the best publicity for a policeman."

"But I thought you said that he beat him with a lamp," I said. "That doesn't sound like an accident to me."

"Well," he said with a smile, "It probably didn't sound like one while he was hitting him either, but it was.

You know how I feel about violence of any kind against any creature, but I think that sometimes not so accidental accidents have to happen to prevent something much worse. In the case that we spoke about, the action was taken with the intent of preventing something terrible, not with the intent of doing something terrible. I doubt that anyone thought about taking a life, only about saving one. Therefore, the taking is accidental, at least to my way of thinking. But then it wouldn't be the first time that I was wrong, but maybe the second."

As he exited the room, Uncle Josh looked back nostalgically, "Thank you for helping me to remember all that you do with these stories. You children are lucky. You have such amazing parents, such an amazing family."

As he started to close the door, a wave of excitement came from the room across the hall.

Ten

While all the storytelling was going on in our room, there was excitement in the twins' room as well. Aunt Sue and Aunt Allie were helping the twins put the finishing touches on a new video game that they invented. They called it "The Sword and the Drag Queen".

The object of the game is for your drag queen to make it through all the pitfalls of getting from Manhattan to the Fire Island Ferry in time to catch the last ferry that will bring you to the Fire Island Drag Queens' Ball. The trick is that you have to arrive in shape to compete for the Miss Drag Queen Crown while traveling on various forms of public transportation, maneuvering around pickets from the Queens Borough Factless Church, dodging in and out of thunderstorms that could easily ruin your makeup, and fending off rival drag queens every step of the way. If you make it all the way in time to make the ferry and get to the other side, you still must face Amy Zorn, the reigning Miss Drag Queen, who is armed with a samurai sword and determined to keep her title. Your only weapons along the way are your high heels, your fully packed makeup case, and a small handbag containing keys, a pen, a mirror, a brush, breath mints, and some pepper spray. Once you use a weapon, you cannot use it again. However, each item in both your makeup case and your small handbag can be used as a separate weapon, providing that you don't use the case or bag first.

Everyone took turns playing the game, but only Aunt Sue made it to the end and won the Miss Drag Queen title, and he did it both times he played. When asked why he was so good at it, he replied, "When it comes to taking out bitches, and getting somewhere looking good, the joysticks only slow me down. But when you get to that big bitch on the other side, remember that the pen is mightier than the sword. It's a fountain pen. I brought her down both times with a squirt to the eye."

Dale did the worst of anyone in the game. "It's not your fault," Aunt Sue tried to console her. "You're a lesbian. What does a lesbian know about makeup? It's the secret to getting past all the other drag queens. Use your makeup to ruin theirs and they freak out. While they run for a mirror, you slip past them. Even a straight rabbi knows that, right Josh?"

"What do you expect?" he replied. "How many years have I known you?"

That night, after all the festivities had ended and we went to bed, there was so much to think about. I thought about the trials and tribulations, not only of the aunts, but of the twins as well. I thought about the amazing game that they invented. I thought about how Robbie was now more like a brother and I was now a writer. I was lost in so many deep thoughts. Then Robbie got undressed and … well … he was naked … so much for the brother part … so much for the deep thoughts.

The next morning it was decided that we were all going to celebrate Robbie's "new forever home" by spending a day in the city. No matter where you live in the New York Metropolitan area, Manhattan is The City. Robbie had never seen Central Park or the Metropolitan Museum, and there was a free "Shakespeare in the Park" performance that evening, so we decided to make a day of it.

When we made it to the Met, we all split up. Mother and Aunts Sue and Allie went to the Alexander McQueen retrospective (Duh!), Uncle Josh and Dad went to the Egyptology exhibits, Chip and Dale went to the African exhibits, and Robbie and I went to see the works of the Impressionists, especially Van Gogh, who was his favorite artist, and coincidentally now mine. Everyone had a great time as we hurried from one great exhibit to the next. There is never enough time to see your fill at the Met, but there's always enough time to leave fulfilled.

We all regrouped in the main lobby in time to grab a couple of famous New York street vendor hot dogs and catch the play in the park. Shakespeare may not always be the perfect way to end an exciting day because not all of Shakespeare is exciting, or even understandable to everyone. However, *A Midsummer Night's Dream* was the play that night, so we had an enchanted evening.

The summer weeks that followed were just as enchanting. The aunts would arrive for the weekend on Friday night, which became either a show night, a game night, or an old movie night. Uncle Josh would arrive on Saturday for a late dinner and stories. And Sunday was Family Day, filled with excursions and picnics and wonderful brunches and dinners.

I particularly loved Saturday nights and Uncle Josh's stories. One of Uncle Josh's stories that particularly stands out was his remembrance of Ruthie, his deceased wife, whom we knew so little about.

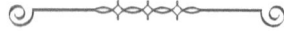

Eleven

"If the story sounds a little egotistical, it's because I was not only a shy young man, but also a little awkward when it came to girls. So if it sounds like Ruthie chased after me, it's because it's true that she did, and it was probably the only way anything was ever going to happen.

Benji and I first noticed Ruthie in our freshman year of high school. I noticed her first. She made sure that I did. Ruthie made it a point to run into me at least two or three times a day. She did anything to get my attention, and I relished hers.

Benji tried to ignore the intrusion at first because he didn't want to appear jealous, which I guess he was. But Ruthie was not one to be ignored. She knew that the best way to get to me was through Benji, and since he was such a likable enough guy, she had no problem developing a friendship that would not only go through him, but also include him.

Developing a friendship with someone who doesn't

want it should have been very difficult, but Ruthie had a sense of humor that was as sharp as Benji's, and she was absolutely fearless. Benji truly admired that. She was on the offense, and he was defenseless. Her irresistibility overwhelmed his resistance, and our friendship soon became a threesome, only platonically of course.

This new friendship was never easy for Benji though. I didn't really understand it at the time. I was not the cleverest young man. I failed to understand that, just as my attraction was naturally turning to girls, Benji, who all along had been focused on boys, had turned his natural attraction to me. But he had always been so discreet about it that I just assumed that it was other boys he was interested in, not me.

Not that it would have made much difference, I suppose, but I never realized that I was in the running. Looking back on it, how insulting would that have been?

Benji must have realized all along the implications of Ruthie and me being both straight and Jewish. He knew where this was heading. I'm sure that he felt that he was the odd man out, not that we ever thought of him that way. But, over the ensuing years in high school, he watched as Ruthie and I became closer and closer until finally he burst one day – not into anger but into tears.

It happened one night after Ruthie had been helping me with my Hebrew studies, something Benji used to do. Benji caught up with us after we had finished, and on our way to grab some coffee, he listened as we laughed and discussed the lessons. This would probably have been difficult enough, but Ruthie let slip in the discussion that we were going to the senior prom. Boom! It must have hit him like a ton of bricks. We were now a couple, and in his mind he was now the odd man out.

He couldn't help it. He simply exploded into tears. 'I love you both. I hope you have a great time, and a great life,' he sobbed as he ran away.

Even then, I was too dense to realize exactly what was going on. I needed Ruthie to explain what I should have understood all along. When she told me how Benji had confidentially confided his feelings toward me with her, I was devastated. I would never have hurt my best friend in any way. For the first time I began to realize in just how many ways I crushed him. Wanting desperately to apologize to him, I tried numerous times to call him.

Benji did not answer his phone and was determined to avoid both Ruthie and me the next day, but Ruthie was Ruthie. She was standing outside his front door when he opened it that morning. She grabbed his arm, yanked him out the door, and dragged him to a nearby coffee shop for 'the talk.'

Benji knew Ruthie was sincere. She promised Benji that if by the end of 'the talk,' he truly wanted her to step out of her relationship with me and away from the friendship the three of us shared, she would. She swore to him that she loved him too much to see him so hurt, and that the last thing she wanted to do was to come between him and me.

'Both Josh and I love you,' she began. 'Josh loves you

more than anyone else on Earth, more than me, I am sure. But his love for you is different than your love for him. He can't help that any more than you can help the way you feel. It's just who you both are.

I could step out of the picture, but that wouldn't change anything between you and Josh. If it's not me, it will eventually be some other girl, one that might have very different plans. The difference is that I want you to always be a part of our lives. Josh needs and wants you in his life, and I do too. The real tragedy in any of this would be if we lost one another.'

Benji wiped away tears as he listened. Not that it made it any easier, but he knew that she was right. After a short pause he said, 'You know that if you marry him, you get me too.'

Ruthie hugged him saying, 'I feel like I already have my first baby. Give Mama a kiss!'

For Benji, it was no longer the beginning of the end, but just the end of the beginning.

Things went pretty smoothly for a while after that. Ruthie and I eventually became engaged. Benji started dating other guys. Maybe not as good-looking as me, but he did the best he could. He was waiting tables. I was busy studying to be a rabbi. True to her word, in whatever free time there was, Ruthie made sure that it included all of us.

When it came time for me to ask Ruthie to marry me, the next fiasco happened … not with Benji, but with my father.

The furor started over the fact that Ruthie and I chose

Benji to be our best man. Now you have to understand that even though my father was seldom there, Benji practically grew up in our home. My father probably loved him as much as he could anyone who was not Jewish and was gay, but that was not very much.

When I told him that Benji would be our best man, he actually said that it was bad enough that this Catholic gay boy consistently seduced me away from my studies into doing God knows what, but now he wanted to embarrass us all by not only breaking Jewish tradition, but probably showing up in a dress. 'Why not just make him the maid of honor?' he asked mockingly.

'No, this will not happen. I forbid it. He can come to the wedding if he dresses properly and stays in the background, but that's it. Your cousin Abraham can be your best man; he's Jewish, and family. That's the way it must be. Period!' My father was fond of saying 'period.'

I was somewhat taken aback, but not that surprised. My father was a strict conservative rabbi, known much more for his keen mind than for his heart. In fact, there were many times when I was convinced that he didn't really have one.

So rather than trying to appeal to some non-existent organ, I simply told him that his period had long since passed. 'Your period is now an exclamation point and it belongs to Ruthie and me.' I said, 'And we place it right after Ben is our best man! Period!'

I watched as the crimson flushed in his face. Before he could say anything, I continued, 'Cousin Abe can be in the wedding party and sign any religious forms that require a Jewish witness, but Ben will be our best man and sign the New York Marriage Certificate. He will be the best man because that is exactly who he is.

I need you to understand,' I continued. 'This is not about you. It's about us, Ruthie and me. Ben is our family, my best friend, and the decision to have him by my side is irrevocable. It is our sincerest wish that you accept this decision, give us your blessing, marry us, and dance and be happy at our wedding. Do you think that you can do that?'

My father was not in the habit of granting wishes. The last time he had an opportunity like this was at my sister Sarah's wedding when she married a Lutheran minister. He not only refused to attend the wedding, he also prevented my mother from attending. It broke her heart.

He wasn't finished. He also declared my sister 'dead' to the family and forbade any further contact with her. Ruthie, Benji, and I attended the wedding, of course. And I kept in regular touch with her, as did my mother secretly. But, due to his stubbornness, they had two grandchildren whom they had never seen. Rose and David were named after my father's parents. The only contact the grandchildren had with the family, outside of me, was the secret telephone calls from my mother.

So it was of little surprise when my father waved our wish away with the same type of stern edict given to my sister. I'll confess that the hurt hung heavy, but I knew that he was wrong, and I was never going to hurt Benji again. I simply said, 'I hope that you are happy with your decision,

Father. Just like the last time, you are the only one who will be." And I left.

When Benji heard about the discussion with my father, he wanted to step aside so that the family would stay together. First, he turned to Ruthie and begged her not to let this ruin her wedding. When she wouldn't listen, he turned to me and pleaded, 'Joshie, don't let something like this come between you and your father. It's not worth it. It's more important …'

'It's more important,' I interrupted, 'that the two people I love the most in the world will be standing next to me on the most important day of my life. The only thing that could ruin our wedding, my friend, is not having you right where you are supposed to be, by my side. Any and all regrets belong to my father.'

That would have been the end of it, but Ruthie had not been heard from yet. Two days before the wedding she burst into my parents' home uninvited.

'If you've come to beg me to attend your wedding, you are wasting your time,' my father shouted.

'Beg you?' Ruthie sneered as she cast aside any attempts at politeness. "Are you really that conceited, that foolish? I've come not to beg you, but to give you one last opportunity to redeem yourself and quit being so stubborn and heartless.'

My father was furious. His face flushed bright red as he screamed, 'You insolent child, who do you think you are to speak to me this way? Have you no respect?'

'Have I no respect? Perhaps you have too much, father,'

she responded. 'Or is it too little for anyone but yourself. Perhaps it is both. Perhaps you have too much respect for whom and what you think you are, and too little respect for everyone else you touch.

And, I'll tell you who I think I am. I think that, like it or not, in two days I will be your daughter, just like the one you so heartlessly discarded. Only unlike your daughter and son, I do not love you as unconditionally as they do. Anyone who receives my love, who gets my respect, has to earn it. And they earn it by giving it back. Do you even know how to do that? I've never seen it. Have your children?' She was on fire.

My father was far too angry to speak and started to storm away from her, but she followed him through the house.

'Your son is already a great man; soon, he will be a great rabbi. Can you not see that? He is loved by all those whom he touches. Can you even understand that? He is wise in both his heart and his mind, and he thinks and decides with both. He understands that a situation cannot be right if everybody suffers. That is the sign of a great teacher, a great rabbi.

When you were right about your daughter's wedding, everybody suffered, including you. They are suffering still. Now you plan to be right again so that there can be more suffering. How wrong can your right be before you can see how wrong it is? It seems to me that the only right that you are expressing is the right to make everybody un-happy. And no one has that right.

And as to your objection to Ben's sexuality, do not presume to know God's heart when you have none of your own. I can assure you that God would find Himself more in Ben's heart than in yours, so where do you think His heart lies? Do not dare to judge that which you cannot live up to.'

My father reached the front door, opened it, and as calm as he was able said to Ruthie, 'I think that you had better leave.'

Ruthie stepped into the doorway and said, 'I will leave. But before I go I will say one more thing. Your son Josh, who loves you, will be at this wedding. Your daughter Sarah, who loves you, will be at this wedding with her husband, Evan, and your two lovely grandchildren, Rose and David, whom you have denied the opportunity to love you, will be there. And Ben, who always looked to you as a father figure, because none existed in his life, will be there.'

Then, as if on cue, my mother stepped into the room and toward the door, suitcase in hand, and said, "Don't forget to mention that his wife, Becky, will also be there.'

My father's face dropped. 'Becky, what do you think you're doing?' he asked, more surprised than demanding.

'I'm mending something that I should never have let tear.' My mother said as she walked through the door. 'And I'm going to my son's wedding to be with my entire family. I wish you the same happiness, husband.' And with that, she grabbed Ruthie's arm and started down the driveway.

Not to be outdone, my father shouted as they left, 'Don't be surprised if the door is locked when you come home.' To which my mother replied, 'Who said anything about coming home?'

My mother stayed at Ruthie's home with Sarah and her family until the day of the wedding. Nothing was heard from my father. We didn't really expect anything else.

Ruthie had arranged for Rabbi Cohen, the rabbi from her parents' temple to perform the ceremony. Everything was so beautiful that day. There was not a detail that Ruthie had missed, all the arrangements, the flowers, the gowns.

My mom sat on one side of the room with Evan and the grandchildren; Sarah was in the wedding party and had not yet made an entrance. Ruthie's family composed the other side of the room, too numerous to even count. Benji, Cousin Abe and I were in the front of the room waiting for the rabbi and the bridal party to arrive. I was a nervous wreck, but Benji was having a grand old time telling jokes, trying to make me laugh.

Then Rabbi Cohen finally arrived. Without saying a word to anyone, he walked up to the front of the room and said, 'I'm afraid that I won't be able to marry this couple today.' Everyone in the room gasped. 'After speaking with Joshua's father, Rabbi Katz, he convinced me that it would be inappropriate for me to officiate on this occasion when …' Just then the side door swung open, and Rabbi Cohen continued, ' … when he is in the room at his son's wedding and requests the honor.'

My father stood sheepishly in the doorway. He looked so different. I had never seen him this way before. He spoke in this sorrowful voice. 'I would like to ask my son's forgiveness; and I humbly ask his permission for the honor …'

Before he could continue, I tearfully shouted, 'Of course Father. Please', and beckoned him to come to the front of the room.

He took a step and said, 'There's more. Do I have the forgiveness and permission of my other son, the best man?'

Benji laughed and cried at the same time, 'Of course, Father. Come! Stop holding up the wedding. Your nervous son here has less than another hour left in him before total collapse.'

My father smiled, threw a kiss toward my mother and the rest of the family and then, with tears in his eyes, hugged Benji and me saying, 'Can you boys ever forgive a foolish old man … '

'Hey this supposed to be a wedding, not "A Christmas Carol."' Benji interrupted. 'If you're going to do the whole Scrooge thing, let's get to the giddy as a drunken man part so we can start celebrating. How wet do we all have to be before we get these people married, anyway?'

My father shook his head and said to me, 'You know. I'd probably love this one even more if I knew what the hell he was saying. Now let's get you married to that tigress. She's a winner, one very smart cookie. Just take my advice. Never get on the wrong side of her. It takes quite awhile to pick up the pieces, believe me.'

So you see, thanks to Ruthie and her indomitable spirit, our whole family was reunited. My father asked for and was given forgiveness from my sister and her family. He and my mother grew closer. He visited and played often with his grandchildren. And a few years later when he died – or excuse me Benji – when he passed on peacefully in his sleep, he did so with a happy heart."

Uncle Josh got up and went to the door and said, "And now, my children, I will say good night."

"But Uncle Josh, what happened to Aunt Ruthie?" I asked. "How did you lose her?"

"One is not so careless with such a gem. I never lost her, not even misplaced. She is here always in my heart. But her passing, dear children, is another story, to be told at another time. Now good night!"

Twelve

That summer was the best summer of my life. I had a whole new family, I began writing prolifically, and I still had Robbie, platonically of course, but hey, I still had Robbie.

Labor Day came and went, and all of a sudden it was school time. The twins and I were in a middle school just down the street from Robbie's new high school. I was soon to turn thirteen and entering the eighth grade. The twins were a year behind in age and grade. And Robbie, who had already turned fourteen, was in his first year of high school. We could all walk to school together, and when Robbie decided to join the football team, Chip, Dale and I would watch him practice after classes.

Besides being a Greek god type and the most stunning player on the team, Robbie was a farm boy with an arm that any professional football player would envy. The coaches took one look at his accurate passing bombs and they knew they had a quarterback.

In Robbie's first year at quarterback, he became a leader, a star, both on and off the field. His team went undefeated due primarily to his play calling and passing prowess. And despite being openly gay, his leadership, coupled with his good looks and personality, made him the most popular kid in school with both sexes. Best of all, through it all, I became his good luck charm, and basked in the glow of being the younger brother who was always by his side.

Of course, my popularity with Robbie's high school crowd didn't always carry over to my middle school crowd. There was one particular boy who it just seemed to irritate. His name was Jimmy Johnson, a known bully. He was the meanest kid in school, and he always traveled around with his goons, the Reed twins, Don and Dave.

I did my best to avoid these three stooges as much as possible, and they always avoided me when I was with Robbie. But one day at school, they caught me unaware, and taunts about my gay dads were angrily exchanged for taunts about Jimmy's lesbian moms and the Reed twins' hillbilly parents. This was not a fight I was looking for. I was going to pay for it.

I'm a definite flight in the whole fight or flight mixture, but the goons made sure that wasn't happening. They each grabbed one of my arms and held me while Jimmy knocked the wind out of me and bent me over with a blow to the stomach. That wasn't enough, though. He blackened my left eye with a right uppercut. I couldn't breathe, or fight back. I felt helpless. As I awaited the next painful blow, something amazing happened. The goons let go of my arms and fell with thuds to the ground, yelling in pain. Almost as quickly, Jimmy was bent over moaning beside me. I was able to catch my breath, and when I looked up Dale was about deliver not one but two blows to Jimmy's soon to be raccoon eyes, and Chip was standing over the Reed twins brandishing one of his famous wooden clogs and threatening to use it again if they even dared move, which they didn't.

Chip and Dale helped me to my feet and walked home with me. As we walked, they explained that they had been watching out for me for a while because they heard that some bullies were targeting me. "I never realized that you had my back," I said thankfully.

"Well, if you'd turn around once in awhile, instead of just looking at Robbie," said Dale, "you would realize that we are always there." I doubt if I ever felt so thankful, and yet so ashamed in my life.

That night at dinner, we had to explain the whole story to Mother and Dad. Mother fussed over my black eye and swollen face, yet scolded me for taunting. "I was just defending you and Dad," I told him, expecting some sort of understanding, if not praise.

"Sweetie, you can't defend and offend at the same time," Mother began. "It was wonderful and brave of you to stand up for your parents, but you can't do so by degrading someone else's parents. They win if you stoop down to their level. You can't throw trash unless you're carrying garbage. You know that. You're better than that."

I knew that Mother was right, but I had as much humiliation as I could stand for one day. So as my parents turned their attention to lauding the twins for defending me, I feigned nausea and dizziness, and asked to be excused. I left the dinner table, slipped into the family room, turned on the TV, and allowed myself to slide into tears.

Not long afterward, Robbie came home from football practice and discovered why I was not at the dinner table. He didn't hesitate. He didn't stop to eat. He came immediately into the family room where I was still sobbing. He slipped out of his sneakers and socks and into the space between me and the sofa. He didn't say a word. He just wrapped his entire body around mine, gently squeezed me tight, and kissed the top of my head. I started sobbing uncontrollably. I'm not even sure why.

"I just …," I started to say.

"I know," he said as he kissed the top of my head again.

"I couldn't even …," I started again.

"It's OK", he whispered. "You don't need to go there. You're OK. It's over. You should never have to go through anything like that. That's not you, that's what makes you so special. I can't even begin to tell you how much it hurts me that you're hurt." He ran his fingers through my hair and continued, "I can't make what happened to you go away, but we can both try to make it better now. Just relax. We don't need to talk about it now. It's over, no explanations, no regrets. Just be. I'm here for you, Hot Stuff, for as long as you need me, I'm here."

I was still sobbing while Robbie was talking, but I don't think that I had ever been happier in my life. Except for a few sniffles, we sat there in silence. Occasionally, he would rub his nose into the back of my neck or stroke my hair, while the TV played something that no one was watching. The warmth of his body and the musk from his practice were so soothing. Eventually, I fell asleep in Robbie's embrace.

When I awoke the next morning, we were lying side by side on the sofa with Robbie's arm around me and a blanket covering us both, most likely a gift from Mother. I was so happy, I didn't move a muscle for another hour or so until Robbie woke. He stretched, kissed the top of my head, and said, "Morning, Sunshine! It's a brand-new day, time to get up."

I had spent the night in Robbie's arms. It was a wonderful new day. I don't even think that I washed the top of my head where Robbie had kissed it. I just spent the day running my fingers through that part of my hair. As silly as that sounds, in retrospect I'd probably do the same today.

The next evening, the parents of everybody involved in the school incident were summoned to the middle school's principal's office with their children. Robbie came along with the rest of us for support.

All the students were forced to wait in the hall outside while their parents met with the principal inside. Outside you could hear the parents arguing. Everyone and no one were to blame depending on who was speaking at the time. Mother and one of Jimmy's mothers were the loudest and most heated. It was starting to get even uglier than the goons when Robbie interrupted the meeting by knocking on the door.

When the principal opened it, Robbie politely apologized for the interruption, "Excuse me, but it sounds like everybody is having a hard time preying nicely. So, before any of you go any further and say anything else that you might regret, you might want to take a look in the hall."

When they did they saw that the two sets of twins, Jimmy and I were all sitting in a circle laughing about raccoon eyes, dirt angels, clog hair and few other funny comments that Robbie made before knocking on the door.

"It's over for them," Robbie said as the adults peered into the hall. "The retention span of kids is even shorter than their attention span. You guys may want to follow suit and shorten your tempers before this stretches into something that's too big to pull back."

Robbie continued. "It's nice and calm out there, so why don't you all make your peace before you step out through the door again." As he turned to walked out the door, he laughed, "And don't make me sit you in a circle."

The principal smiled the smile of a convict who had just been reprieved. He thanked Robbie for a great job with the students. He asked the parents and children to go home and think about what they had all learned. I'm not sure that he even knew or believed in what he was saying, but I know that he was glad when everyone listened and left.

The next weekend, there was much to tell the aunts and Uncle Josh. Aunt Sue loved the clog story so much that he talked about making a comeback with the clogs in the act.

Aunt Allie wasn't quite as enthused, probably realizing that he would most likely be the clog recipient. Uncle Josh made a point of telling Robbie how proud he was of the way Robbie diffused the whole situation in the principal's office.

"I hope that someday you'll have the opportunity to work with children," he said. "And I hope that they will take the opportunity to learn from you. You're a natural! It's a rare gift, especially in one so young. You have many gifts. I hope that you don't let this one get lost in the shuffle."

Later that night, we again all retired to our usual stations and places, with the exception of Robbie who left for a late practice. I missed Robbie, but it was nice to have Uncle Josh all to myself. I asked him if he would mind continuing the story of Aunt Ruthie's passing. I promised that I would relate the story to Robbie when he got home so he wouldn't have to tell it again. He seemed a little more hesitant than usual, but with a huge sigh, he began.

"As you know from many of our conversations, Ruthie was an extremely strong woman, both emotionally and spiritually," he said as his eyes noticeably moistened. "Physically, however, she was much frailer than any of us had understood. Her heart had always been too big and full of love for such a small body. And, on the day that our son was born, it was sorely tested. And it either passed, or failed that test, depending on how you look at it. In retrospect, I think it passed with honors."

The shocked look on my face revealed that I didn't understand the answer and had never heard of his son.

"I see that there is still much to tell," he continued. "Yes,

I have a son. His name was, or rather is, Jacob. That was the middle name of my father, who, as you know, was also a rabbi, and had passed on shortly before Ruthie became pregnant. With so many dead relatives to choose from, and considering the stormy relationship I had with my father, choosing any part of his name was not so easy. But Ruthie insisted on Jacob. And as always, she won, but only on the day before Jacob was born. I am not as easy as people think.

We did not know before Ruthie became pregnant, that childbirth would be dangerous for her, so we planned on a large family. Only God in His infinite wisdom knows how things would have been different had we known. Needless to say, we didn't, and there was no turning back for Ruthie.

That's the strangest thing about mothers, my son. There are perhaps no braver warriors on Earth than mothers who truly want to raise a family. They're fierce, and they can and will face anything on their march toward motherhood.

So, despite many difficulties, and believe me there were many, Ruthie loved, protected and nurtured the child inside her womb until at last he made his grand entrance into the world with one loud beautiful cry. I can still hear it to this day. My heart soared as he cried to the world, "I am." It was one note, and yet, such a beautiful symphony.

Then suddenly the music stopped. As quickly as he came into this world, Jacob left it. He just left! No noise, no reason, nothing. He just quietly left.

In shock I turned to Ruthie, who had tears in her eyes.

I didn't know what to say. But it didn't matter. No one had to tell her. She knew. More than I imagined, she knew.

She took my hand and tearfully whispered, 'I love you, Josh. Forgive me. I'm sorry.'

Before I could even tell her that there was nothing to forgive, that there was no reason for her to be sorry, that there was nothing more that she could do, and that she was the heroine in this sad story, she closed her eyes. And then in horror, it hit me. It was not for Jacob that she was sorry. It was for me. Her heart was too big and their bond too strong for her to let Jacob go alone. As quickly as he left, Ruthie left to take care of him.

I think that she knew that eventually, I would be all right, but she couldn't take the chance that he would be. And so, in what seemed like a flash, my wife and my son went into the Light and left me in utter darkness.

How desperately I wanted to join them. I was alone in absolute despair.

Miraculously, Benji showed up and dragged me from the delivery room. I was inconsolable, and he was kind enough to not even try. He just held me in his arms as the tears from my pain and heartbreak poured out all over him. As you can imagine, it was the darkest hour of my life.

And yet, though it seemed no flame on earth could brighten such darkness, in the very next room, within the very same hour, a miracle was being born: You. Your mother gave birth to a new light in the world even in the midst of the darkness and despair next door. That's why

Benji was there. It was because of you that he was able to come to my rescue."

In retrospect, it was a foolish thing to ask at the time, but I was young and caught up in the moment. "Do you think that I might be Jacob, Uncle Josh? I mean, do you think that his spirit, or soul, or whatever, could have gone into my mother and became me? Could we possibly be the same spirit, and that's why you often call me son?"

Later, I would realize that he did not seem as puzzled by the question as you might think. He just smiled and hugged me as only one who loves his child would do. "I believe that you are you, my child. Beyond that, I am wise enough to know that I am not wise enough to know anything more. Not questioning the workings of the Creator gives me the appearance of wisdom. I am content with that.

A wise man said that, 'Even God should be allowed his secrets.'"

"What wise man said that?"

"I just did," he laughed. "Weren't you listening? What – do you think I make necklaces with these pearls?"

Your uncles, I should say your parents, because they are certainly that and more, have been gracious enough to allow me to be a part of your life and theirs. For that privilege, I am eternally grateful. I call you son partly because I am older than you, and we are family. But mostly, I call you son because I couldn't be prouder of you, nor love you any more if you were a child of mine. I call you son, because it gives me great joy and honor to do so!"

As Uncle Josh stood up to leave, he closed his eyes for

a minute then said, "I'd like to think that you and Jacob would have been good friends and would have been as close as Benji and I."

"Uncle Josh," I said as I felt the warmth of Jacob's presence in my life for the first time. "We are!"

He left to tears in both our eyes.

When Robbie returned home later that evening, I did my best to retell Uncle Josh's story of Jacob and Aunt Ruthie as accurately as possible. When I was finished, Robbie appeared very touched by the story and remarked that I too was a great storyteller. "But I have to admit," he confessed. "Nothing adds to a story more than Uncle Josh's Jewish expressions and intonations. You know what I mean? It's just not the same."

Oy Vey! What is he kvetching about? Is he kibitzing? Talk about chutzpah. I was farklempt. Who knew he needed expressions and intonations? What am I, chopped ad libber?

That night I thought about Jacob and how I was sure that we would have been good friends. I wasn't sure of the best way to tell him that, so I wrote the following story for him.

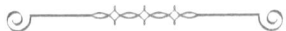

Thirteen

IMAGINE

By Gene Poole-Hall

(Age 13)

Reality is not all it's cracked up to be. This is a good thing, for it is within the cracks of reality that true magic is found. Sam found his magic there in the form of his best friend Bobby. Bobby is magical because only Sam seems to know he's there. He's always been there. Sam's known Bobby for as long as he can remember. They've never been apart. They're best friends. They've grown up together.

Sam knows that, like him, Bobby is the only child of loving parents. They would often discuss and compare each other's parents when their own parents weren't around. Sam's parents didn't discourage their friendship or the conversations in the beginning because they thought it was better to encourage Sam's imagination, especially since he was alone so much of the time. But after a while his parents began to feel that it was getting a little worrisome. He was getting older. Soon he would be in school. Now his parents were beginning to worry that they had let things go too far. It was time for Bobby to leave. It was time for real friends.

Sam's parents tried to explain to him that Bobby wasn't real. He wasn't really there. He was just someone that Sam had made up in his mind. That was fun when he was little, but he's bigger now and it was time for friends just like him, friends who were real.

His parents' explanation made no sense to Sam because, even though he and Bobby were different, and only they could see each other, they knew that each other was real. They played together all the time, shared each other's secrets, and explored each other's worlds together. That's pretty real. Otherwise, they must both be imaginary, and have made each other up at the same time, and that's how they became real.

Anyway, if there was one thing that Sam was sure of it was that they were both real now, really real. And that's all that really mattered.

Sam's parents tried desperately to get him to become friends with other children his age, real children like him. Sam didn't mind this, but only if Bobby could come, too. Sam's parents agreed hoping that when Sam was with the other children that Bobby wouldn't show up. He did.

The play situation did not play out so well, as the other children apparently didn't see or believe in Bobby either. They teased Sam about his invisible friend. And the more they teased him, the more convinced Sam became that Bobby was truly his only friend, the only real friend he ever needed. And that was just fine with him. So he and Bobby stopped playing with the other children. They didn't need them. They still had each other.

Next, Sam's parents took him to see someone who asked him a lot of questions about Bobby. He seemed a bit more understanding. He told Sam's parents that Sam's imagination was very impressive and should not be discouraged. It will serve Sam well someday, he said, and he will outgrow the imaginary friendship. Instead, he told them to keep Sam completely occupied with adventures that only the three of them could share. Eventually Sam would forget about Bobby, he said, and the imaginary friend would simply go away.

That didn't work either. Sam and Bobby simply kept quiet about Bobby tagging along on the adventures, and Bobby got to enjoy them, too.

Eventually, it came time to go to school, and they had to be apart for most of the day. That was OK with them, though, because they knew that they would be back together later in the day, and that they would have even more to talk about, even more experiences to share.

Sam liked to tell Bobby about his day, but his experiences seemed rather boring compared to Bobby's. Bobby's day just seemed so much more exciting. It was almost unimaginable to Sam, because Bobby's world was so different, so unusual.

Sam had seen this world often through Bobby's eyes,

but never through his own. And he wondered what it would be like to see it and feel it the way Bobby did. What would it even be like to feel something, anything, whatever that meant?

Sam wondered if his parents could even imagine a world like Bobby's: a world where the people and the things around them were something called solid, which meant things they could feel. These solids had things called shapes. The people even had shapes themselves. Could his parents imagine shapes? Could they imagine that there were things that you could not pass through, things that you lived inside of, things that you needed to get around in, things that grew, things that didn't, things?

Imagine, he thought. Just imagine.

And he continued to.

Fourteen

Our second summer together as a family was every bit as wonderful as the first. We went on our first family vacation together to Provincetown on Cape Cod. Uncle Josh was the only member of the family who didn't join us because he had Sabbath services and never ate seafood. Provincetown is famous for many things, and seafood is right up there.

Mother and the aunts often worked the clubs along Commercial Street during the summers, so they were still pretty well known and popular. But nobody was more popular than Robbie who managed to turn just about every head as he walked the street in his beach clothes and sandals. It was pretty understandable. He may have been only fifteen, but he was still a 10.

We spent the balance of our mornings and early afternoons at the beach. Mother and Dad would sit under their multicolored umbrellas reading and socializing with the neighbors of the day. The aunts tagged along, but were so covered in hooded terry robes under their umbrellas that they looked like sand phantoms hiding from any ray of sun sure to shrivel them. And Robbie, Chip, Dale and I spent the days swimming, boarding and lathered in so much of Mother's sunblock that for two days the sun didn't even come out at all.

Late afternoons were teatime at any one of the many outdoor restaurants, usually some variation of Long Island Iced Tea for the adults and lobster rolls and soda for the rest of us. It was at these afternoon stops that Mother, Aunt Sue and Aunt Allie would usually meet one or two of their former fellow performers, or sometimes just someone who recognized them from their acts. You might think that the conversations would get boring for the rest of us, but we would pick up some pretty interesting information, and even a dessert or two, from the visitors along the way.

One of the more interesting stories involved Mother and a fake feud with a performer whose name I think was Peggy Lee. It seems that when things ran slow in places like the Kit Kat Club, performers would call on friends to help out with publicity, usually a tidbit that would be picked up in the tabloids. Peggy Lee was in the audience on a night that Mother was impersonating her. After a few choruses of one of her more famous numbers, Miss Lee apparently stood up and shouted, "I don't sound like that." To which Mother replied, "No, but keep practicing, Honey; you'll get there." Peggy walked over to the exit, swung open the door, turned around and shouted,

"I'm out of here! I've never been so humiliated in my life."

"Are we talking me or the dress, Sweetie?" Mother called as she left.

The next morning the two friends read the newspaper blurbs over brunch.

There was also an interesting story about Aunt Sue and a decidedly drunk patron. Apparently the patron led Sue to believe that he was interested in him. After his performance, Sue went over to this guy's table and started a conversation. After a few drinks the guy started to sound a bit abusive, so Sue started to leave. The guy stopped him and asked, "So what's this crap about Japanese Delight? You're obviously black as the ace of spades!"

Sue maintained his composure, and said, "While I'm extremely proud of my skin color, I am also descended from Japanese royalty, so my color is somewhat illusionary."

"Yeah right!" the drunkard replied, "Do you know the difference between illusionary and delusionary?"

"That would be your sex life." Sue replied.

Apparently the guy got angry and took a swing at Sue, but missed. Allie, who had just come on stage for his Dietrich number, leapt on top of the guy's back as he continued to move toward Sue. Since Allie couldn't stop him in that position, he tried to jump off the guy's back, but his Velcro corset somehow attached to the guy's belt. While Allie was riding bronco, Mother, on hearing all the commotion, ran out from backstage, grabbed hold of the guy, and threw him out the front door with Allie still attached. "It was one of the best rides of my life." Allie said. "And I rode him until he was busted!"

Not all the afternoon conversations, however, were pleasant stories or encounters. Some people don't know how to bring that to the table. One of the local performers was like that. One of the first things that he did when he arrived uninvited at our table was to ask Aunt Sue if he recognized anyone in town who he hadn't slept with. Aunt Sue passed off the jab with, "Lots, Darling. I'm actually very discreet. I never sleep with anyone who absolutely refuses to sleep with me. You should try it some time when you're not wearing your Bermuda shorts triangle. They give you more of a rag queen than a drag queen persona."

As if that wasn't enough, the rude guy then actually asked Aunt Allie if he was still sleeping with his hunky brother Mohammed. That got him a cold drink in the face and a stern lecture from Mother as Aunt Allie stormed away.

"Do you believe that queen just did that to me?" the guy asked incredulously as though the lecture never happened.

"Look at the bright side," Mother responded sternly. "Your cologne just improved three notches. You do know that Eau de Toilette doesn't really come from there, don't you?"

"My cologne happens to be very expensive."

"I can imagine. Those gas stations really do overcharge," Mother assured him.

"But Eau de Hoboken does suit you so well," Aunt Sue added as the guy got up to leave. "Look under the table before you go, Baby. You may have left a shred of dignity behind. Oh, no! My mistake, there's none left."

The interesting part to the rest of us was that Mother's lecture was about the rudeness of bringing up the topic of sleeping with Mohammed, not about whether or not there was any truth to it. As interesting as it was, though, we all knew better than to ever go there. And we never did.

There was one other annoying aspect to the afternoon teas. Robbie did get a couple of tea dance proposals the few times that we were sitting apart from the adults. The interested guys were usually twice his age, very flirtatious, and sexy. I could tell that he was flattered, maybe even interested, but thankfully he let Mother handle the proposals with a stern "Oh, no! You did not just try to pick up my fourteen-year-old child." Robbie was actually fifteen at the time, but Mother thought that fourteen sounded like more jail time.

I love Mother! Somehow I felt as if I was the one who he was protecting at the time.

As exciting as the mornings and afternoons were, nothing compares to Provincetown at night. We had dinner at a different restaurant every evening. Clam chowder, Portuguese kale soup, oysters, lobster and all sorts of fresh seafood were on tap everywhere, and Mother and Dad let us have our fill, and then some.

Then after dinner there was always some fabulous type of show we had never seen before. There were even some that Robbie, Chip, Dale and I weren't supposed to get into, but Mother and the aunts had pull, so we always did.

Normal?

We were able to see our first drag shows that didn't involve Mother or the aunts, which were performed on a real stage. We heard comedians who told jokes and said things that we had to promise not to repeat, even to each other. We enjoyed some excellent singers, and a few that were not so, and there was even a fantastic magic act.

Best of all, I got to bond with Chip and Dale, both of whom I had ignored far too long in my obsession with Robbie. We all became a great team. We became a real family … in all ways … for always!

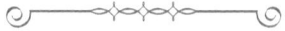

Fifteen

I know they say that time passes quicker as you get older, but it's amazing how quickly summer turns to bummer when you're young and back in school. The cool difference this time, though, was that I was starting high school, the same high school that Robbie attended.

I had a great advantage over most of the freshman class in that most of Robbie's friends, who were sophomores and juniors, knew me. I got to hang out with Robbie and a more popular crowd. When other freshman got picked on by upperclassmen they would often come to me to ask for help. I'd talk to Robbie who could usually solve the problem. That in turn made me more popular in the freshman class, too. I learned to love high school very quickly.

Chip and Dale both had soccer practice at their middle school, and I made it a point to watch their practices as well as Robbie's. If they could have my back, the least I could do was to back them. I was never really into sports so I only watched when any of them were on the field. The remainder of the time I'd be either studying or writing. And if the truth be known, while I was watching them, I'd still be thinking about studying or writing.

I considered myself fortunate that I never had to actively participate in school sports because of a slight heart murmur, which may have developed at the mere thought of having to participate in school sports. Robbie, Chip and Dale, however, were all very athletic and genuinely enjoyed playing their respective sports.

Not everybody on the fields enjoyed their enthusiasm, though, and it was while also observing my challenged peers that I wrote the following story. It was not the best story I had ever written, but I had hoped that it would get across the idea that when it comes to participation, choice should be important.

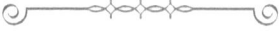

Sixteen

THE LOTTERY

By Gene Poole-Hall

(Age 14)

Not all planets are like ours. In fact, some are so different that the lives of their occupants seem like science fiction to us. Hermes' planet is like that. Most of its inhabitants are androgynous. It appears almost as though they were descended from the bees on our planet. Only in this case, there is just one lucky bee that gets to mate with a do-it-yourself queen.

The Creator, or queen, on Hermes planet is chosen by lottery. The winner of the lottery gets to choose a mate that will help produce the entire planet's offspring for a period of time similar to an Earth year.

The approaching lottery was never something that Hermes would have wanted to enter. Being shy and somewhat of a loner, he was more than content in his solitude.

He was content to be whom and what he was, and nothing more. The problem was that this lottery was not a choice.

When you reached your twentieth year, the lottery was compulsory. Hermes' group just turned twenty years. Like it or not, he and everyone else in his group were about to be entered.

Of course, not everybody in Hermes' birth year felt the way that he did about the lottery. Most members thought of it as an honor, a duty, a service to the populace of their planet that no one would ever think of refusing. Hermes understood honor and service; he just wanted someone else to experience it. In that respect, he was very different, but with no right of refusal, that difference didn't make any whatsoever.

Now, looks can be deceiving on any planet. But when everyone in every cycle looks exactly alike, the confusion may be compounded by more than a little. The inhabitants of Hermes' planet had to rely on small personality variances to determine who is who, and what is what. It was never an easy task, as they were all profoundly affected by the heretofore rather indistinguishable participants in their original birth year.

Hermes' group was different, however. It was unknown at that time, but one of the participants in his birth year had a multiple personality disorder. Nothing like this anomaly had ever happened before. And Hermes' planet had never experienced variances like the one it produced. Everyone born in Hermes' year was dissimilar. Their strengths and personalities differed, and oddly enough these variances made them look far less homogeneous than the rest of the population. So, what they brought to this particular lottery was bound to be different.

For Hermes' planet, the disparities in his group's personalities would soon be of great concern. His planet was falling behind the other planets in its sector. They needed a lottery winner who understood the importance of choosing the right companion personality for the next birth year. They needed a change, and they needed it now.

Because of the uncertainties, this year was going to be the planet's biggest challenge. And worst of all, it was about to be played out under this new lottery system.

Before the lottery, which was only in its second cycle, this might have been less of a concern. The participants for each twentieth cycle were chosen by the elders. There was more control, and selection was fairly simple since there weren't major personality differences.

Still, the old selection process seemed a bit too contrived, too planned. And it appeared that the offspring it produced were growing weaker, rather than stronger, as anticipated. So it was finally decided to open the possibility of participation to everyone in each maturing birth year in the hope that the addition of random selection might add an unforeseen - and more positive element.

It was too early to judge the results of the first lottery cycle, so the second was about to take place with Hermes obviously in the mix. As you might expect, his enthusiasm underwhelmed him more than usual.

There was so much to think about now. The lottery

winner's life not only was about to vastly change, but so too was his appearance. He would never look or be the same again.

Plus, although there were some pleasant rumors, no one ever spoke about what happened to the winner once the offspring they created had matured. Added to all this was the responsibility that the winner must also pick a partner from all the other personalities in his cycle. And that pick, that companion choice, would have the most profound effect on the next ensuing cycle.

Hermes didn't want the win, he certainly didn't want the change, and he didn't want the responsibility of having to choose the right partner. But when his name was picked, it didn't really matter what he wanted. He didn't really have a voice; he didn't really have a choice. The future depended on him. Everything was about to change.

Hermes had one moon to prepare himself and choose his partner. In one moon he must drink the sacred nectar that would change his body forever. Hermes would never again look like everyone else. He would become a Creator, the architect of the next cycle, his planet's most important responsibility. The change would allow him to conceive the next cycle after mating with his partner during the Begetting Ceremony.

Once he conceives, he will then retire to the cloistered Sanctuary of the Creators where he will spend the rest of his life with his predecessors from previous years. He doesn't know it yet, but he will be very happy.

Hermes will nurse and care for his prodigy until they

are healthy enough to leave the cloister. After they leave, he will not see any of them again until it comes time for one of them to also join the cloister as a Creator.

Hermes set about the task of trying to determine the best partner for the ceremony. Each birth year consists of ten offspring, so Hermes must choose his partner from the remaining nine in his year.

Thoron is strong and bold; his offspring would add strength and protection to all the cycles. Albert is brilliant; his offspring could add much to the understanding of the nature of things on their planet. Leonardo is inventive, and his heirs could bring about important changes in technology. Michael is artistic, and his prodigy could bring about a renaissance in their culture. Everyone really likes Phil, so his heirs would be great boosts in the areas of diplomacy and politics, and he would probably be the most popular choice. Norm and Joe are extremely pleasant, but probably wouldn't have much of an effect on a future generation. That leaves only Judge, who is supercritical of everything, and the studious Sage, who is, by far, the wisest of them all, but not very popular, as nobody listens to wisdom anymore.

Hermes was confused. Many of the choices had positive effects in one direction or another, but which one was the best? He decided to ask Sage. After all, he is wise. Perhaps he would know and reveal who the best choice really is.

Sage listened to Hermes' dilemma, and understood his confusion. The planet's inhabitants had always been taught to follow the will of others, never to lead, never to choose for themselves. Choosing meant leading, thinking for oneself. With the exception of the elders, this was an alien concept to the planet.

Sage told Hermes that, in order for the new system to work, he must determine for himself what he thinks the planet needs most, and then pick a partner who he thinks will help to accomplish that. This is a once in a lifetime opportunity.

If Hermes feels that a strong defense is needed, he might choose Thoron. If he feels that science or technology are more important, he might choose either Albert or Leonardo. If the soul of the populace requires uplifting, he could choose Michael. But the important thing he must do if there ever is to be change is that he must make the decision himself.

Sage asked Hermes to remember one thing when making his choice. "Remember what it feels like to not have a choice and then consider what it feels like when you do. Your future offspring will know the thoughts and feelings of both you and your partner. You are writing the recipe for change."

Hermes knew that Sage was wise, and he felt that he would make the right decision if he carefully heeded Sage's advice. All night long, he weighed the choices over and over again, making one decision, then another, and weighing the consequences of each. By the morning of the next moon, he was sure that he had made the right choice.

He was sure that what the planet needed was not a cycle that would merely follow someone else's decision, but one that would help everyone to choose the right decision for themselves. Then everyone could choose if and how to participate. Someday, there could even be more than two participants at a time. Perhaps the Creators would even be free to once again mingle with the rest of the cycles.

If Hermes' choice was right, and he was sure it was, there would be few lotteries to follow his. The cycles actually would learn to think, act, and most importantly, choose for themselves. He and his choice for a partner would have led the way.

He made the wisest choice he could make. He chose Sage.

Seventeen

Robbie's team went undefeated again his second year, and he was starting to draw the attention of some major colleges. His picture appeared in the local newspapers a number of times, and our room filled with trophies and framed clippings attesting to his success. I loved it. Every night I had the local hero all to myself.

I was fourteen, and I was starting to really feel my oats. Actually I had been feeling them for a long time just being around Robbie, but now I wanted to know how to sow and reap some of them.

I couldn't talk to Robbie because that was the field I had in mind for sowing and reaping. I certainly didn't want to tempt the teasing of Chip and Dale, who were well aware of my feelings. Everyone would know everything if I risked talking to the aunts. I was sure it would embarrass Uncle Josh far more than it would me if I asked him. That left me with the choice of talking to either Mother or Dad. I chose the more embarrassing.

I figured that the best way to broach the whole sex thing with Mother was to ask about dating.

"Did you date many men before you met Dad?" I asked Mother one night while helping to prepare dinner.

"No, Sweetie!" he responded. "Most of them were pretty well dated by the time I got to them."

"You know what I mean. Did you go out a lot?

"Every day. I'm not a hermit you know."

"Cute," I said. "Did you see a lot of guys?"

"What am I, blind? Of course I saw lots of guys."

"Are we playing chess?" I asked.

"That depends. Are we having a sex talk?"

"And if the answer is yes?" I asked.

"Then we're playing chess."

"I just want to know when I'm ready," I said.

"Oh Sweetie, don't worry. I'll tell you in a few years when you're ready. Until then, go set the table."

"But it's important." I said as I grabbed the silverware.

"I know, Sweetie. That's why I want you to set it."

I continued to mutter under my breath, but it still drew a response.

"Genie, you know I have a hearing problem. I can still hear you. You know it's not nice to fool around with Mother's nature."

Later that night, obviously at Mother's urging, Dad gave me the talk about how important it was not to rush into things. He said that sex is an important part of a relationship, but only when you're old enough to commit to one. The first time in particular should be very special because you will remember it the rest of your life. And then he warned me about how dangerous sex can be if you're not careful, and the terrible diseases that you could wind up with when you're not. There were more holes than fillers in the conversation that he was obviously uncomfortable having. When he left, I was more confused than before he started. My loaded weapon was apparently more dangerous than I thought.

I can't say that I was glad we had the talk. Especially when, a few weeks later, on yet another night of unbridled throbbing while watching Robbie walk around the room naked, I had my first orgasm. I didn't know what happened. I didn't understand why. It just happened. It never happened before. And I didn't know what to do.

It happened as Robbie was walking into our bathroom, and as far as I could tell, he didn't seem to see or hear anything. I tried to quickly clean up, but the room had a strong smell, almost like bleach. So I grabbed everything, ran downstairs to the laundry room, hid all the evidence until I could dispose of it, washed up, and returned to the room with Robbie apparently already asleep in bed.

As I slid into bed, I realized that I obviously wasn't careful, so I spent the night wondering what disease I might have contacted. Even worse, I didn't want to be the cause of Robbie catching anything. I was afraid that some of my sperm had wiggled their way over to his bed.

Needless to say, my oats had been plowed under for a while.

Eighteen

That summer, we persuaded Uncle Josh to join us on a vacation that we all could enjoy. We decided to fly to Seattle and rent a minibus big enough for all of us to take our time driving down the West Coast through Los Angeles to San Diego.

We spent a few days exploring Seattle before setting out on a journey that, with the aunts in the bus, we knew would be reminiscent of *Priscilla Queen of the Desert*.

Mother, Aunt Sue, and Aunt Allie did all the planning with layovers for exploring in Portland, Ashland (for the Shakespeare festival, of course), Eureka, San Francisco, San Luis Obispo, Los Angeles, and San Diego. They booked three rooms in every stop with the occupants divided the same way they would be if we were home. Mother and Dad were always in the smallest room; Robbie, Uncle Josh, and I in the next size up; and the twins and the aunts in the largest room, which usually doubled as the family room.

Seattle, our first stop, was exciting. We spent three days exploring the Space Needle, the Aquarium, the Monorail, the Seattle Art and Seattle Asian Art Museums, Pioneer Square, and of course Pike Place Market. The market was particularly exciting since Aunt Sue insisted on catching one of the huge fish that the fishmongers throw, and wound up sprawled on the ground buried under a fish that was almost as big as him. I won't go into the off-color jokes he made, but we were delayed while he ran back to the hotel to change. (Dad caught the fish picture on his camera and it remains on the refrigerator to this day under the caption, "Sue Sheed By The One That Didn't Get Away.)

After Seattle, we took the coastal road down to Portland, where we explored Lan Su Chinese Garden, the Portland Japanese Garden (for Aunt Sue), the Jewish Museum (for Uncle Josh), Voodoo Doughnut (for everyone), Powell's City of Books, and the Portland Saturday Market. Actually, we explored Voodoo Doughnut twice. There's magic in the people who do Voodoo.

Next on our trip was Ashland and the Shakespeare Festival. Mother and the Aunts had arranged not only tickets for *A Midsummer Night's Dream*, but costumes as well. Robbie and I were Lysander and Demetrius in very sexy open shirts and tight pants; Dad and Mother were Oberon and Titania in fairy splendor; Aunt Sue was Hippolyta the Amazon Queen; Uncle Josh was Duke Theseus; Aunt Allie was extremely cute as Mustardseed; Chip never looked better as Puck; and Dale, who had her choice between Hermia and Peter Quince, of course chose the carpenter.

We went to the performance in full regalia. There were even a few people along the way who asked for autographs, thinking that we were most assuredly cast members. For the most part our costumes rivaled or were better than those on stage. As Aunt Sue observed, "What do you expect when there are real fairies at work?"

Our next stop was Eureka where we saw the redwoods and visited Humboldt Bay during a short layover.

Then it was on to San Francisco where it is impossible to see everything you want to see. We visited Fisherman's Wharf where we took trolleys, and The Market where we took streetcars. We visited Chinatown, Japantown, Golden Gate Park at sunset, the Castro, and the Embarcadero. We took side trips to Napa Valley and Yosemite National Park; and on the trip out, spent a day visiting Monterey and Carmel. It was easy to see how anyone could leave their heart in San Francisco.

Next on the tour was San Luis Obispo from which we took side trips to Hearst Castle and a few of the surrounding missions. We also visited Bubblegum Alley, a seventy-foot-long alley known for its accumulation of used bubble gum left by visitors. Aunt Sue swore that he would never chew again, or as Chip remarked, "This really, really blows!"

LA, here we come, lots of traffic, sprawling sites and glitz ahead. We toured Hollywood, went to Disneyland, Venice Beach, Grauman's Chinese Theatre, the Hollywood

Bowl for a Philharmonic concert, Dodger Stadium when the Giants were in town, the Getty Center, and the Griffith Observatory. We did tours of the stars' mansions, a few movie studios, and of course the artistic treasures of Pasadena. We were all having a great time, but it was very hot and Los Angeles is a hard city to navigate. It's easier to lose your mind than your heart there.

The last stop on the tour was San Diego where we hit the beaches and visited the sites in a much more relaxed manner. Besides blocking out the sun once again with Mother's SPF 1000 sunblock, we took our time visiting the Gaslamp Quarter, Old Town, the San Diego Zoo, and the Anza-Borrego Desert.

We thought about crossing the border to Tijuana on one of our last days, but the aunts said that they couldn't go there. When we asked why, Aunt Sue said, "Oh! Honey, you do not want to go there." We weren't sure if he meant the town or the explanation, so we didn't.

Nineteen

If there is anything that time respects less than age, it's endless fun. If you are enjoying life, time passes in the blink of an eye. One minute we were having fun and the next we were back in school. Our days were once again filled with classes and clubs, and practices and homework. The exciting part was that Chip and Dale became freshmen in our high school. We were all together again.

During the school year, Robbie and I ran for junior and sophomore class president. We both won, Robbie because he was a football hero with a great personality, and me because I was his straight A brother. (I don't actually think that the straight A's helped all that much.)

Mother and Dad were so proud of us that they offered to get us congratulation presents. "I know that you're sixteen now," Mother said to Robbie. "But don't go thinking anything crazy like a car. There's plenty of time for that when you're thirty or so. Think of something a little more personal and safe like a bike, with a helmet and kneepads and God knows what else."

"Actually, I have been thinking about something for a long time. You've always treated me like a family member. You're the only family I ever really had. And I hope you know how much I love you all. If you guys are up for it, the best present you could possibly give me is to officially adopt me into the family. You know ... the whole deal: the name, the certificate, everything. I would just love it."

Tears were swelling all around at Robbie's request. Mother, who had been standing over the stove cooking, dropped the pot he was holding and ran over to Robbie, "What color car did you say you wanted, Sweetie?"

"Well son, I think you have your answer," said Dad. "But I hope you realize that your new last name will be Poole-Hall."

"I can't think of a better place for that name to hang, Dad," Robbie smiled.

In the wave of emotion and excitement of the moment, they forgot to ask me what I really wanted. I looked over at Robbie beaming. It was OK. They couldn't give me that anyway.

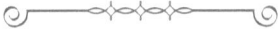

Twenty

Robbie's adoption went smoothly. Although it really didn't change anything between us, it was comforting to know that he would officially be around for quite awhile. I thought of it as insurance on my love life, even if I didn't have one.

Robbie continued to excel in football. With him at the helm at quarterback, his team was within one game of a third consecutive undefeated season. Although there would still be a senior year to complete, the final game had more than twenty college level scouts to watch him play.

The opposing team was also undefeated. They played evenly most of the game until two costly fumbles put our team behind by five points with less than a minute to play. Robbie calmly led his team downfield. He had one shot at the end zone with two seconds on the clock. The opposing team rushed the passer. Robbie scrambled. He released the ball just as he was being tackled. The ball landed perfectly in the hands of one of our receivers. Touchdown! We had won the game.

The crowd rushed the field. Everyone was jumping up and down. Then we realized that Robbie and his tackler were still on the ground. Both boys were rolling around in pain. His tackler was holding his knee. Robbie was holding his passing arm. Both teams rushed to help their player. Despite the obvious pain, Robbie insisted on walking off the field in celebration with his teammates.

Once inside the locker room, Mother, Dad and his coach rushed Robbie to the hospital. They could tell that his arm was in bad shape. The only question was how bad.

X-rays revealed multiple breaks and fractures. He would have to be operated on immediately. The good news was that it would heal and he would regain full use of his arm again. The bad news was that he would never have the same strength and range that he had before, and the repairs would ultimately be too fragile for him to continue playing football.

Robbie took the news the way you would expect he might. "Well, if I'm ever going to get into college now, I'd better kick-start my brain. Looks like we have our work cut out for us, Hot Stuff."

Robbie's operation went as planned, and he had to stay overnight in the hospital. The next morning, he had a surprise visitor. It was Mark, the player from the opposing team who had tackled him.

Mark arrived on crutches, but still able to carry flowers, candy and a few newspaper clippings of Robbie's finest moment. He had tears in his eyes as he tried to apologize for the tackle. Robbie told him that it wasn't anybody's fault. It was a clean tackle, just a bad break, literally.

Mark confessed to Robbie that he never liked to play football, but played to please his father who was a big fan. He hardly ever got into the game because of his weight and slender build, and that was just fine with him. But when he saw Robbie, and was actually put into the game, he tried desperately to introduce himself in the only way open to him. He somehow slipped past the blockers and made his first tackle, "It was the only one I ever really wanted to make," he confessed. "I just had to meet you somehow. Being on top of you seemed like a perfect opportunity."

"I have a phone number and e-mail address," Robbie laughed. "There are less painful ways for both of us, but I'm happy for the introduction."

Mark and Robbie talked and laughed through the rest of the morning until it came time for our family to pick Robbie up and bring him home. I could tell that something was up by the way they looked and smiled at each other as we gathered Robbie's things. My suspicions were confirmed when, as we were leaving, Robbie flashed a "call me" sign with the fingers on his good hand.

That might have been the end of it if Miss Congeniality had only read the "Please Be Quiet" sign. But if it ain't one thing, it's a Mother. "Would your friend like to come over and have lunch with us?" Mother asked Robbie as we were leaving.

"Robbie probably needs his rest," I interjected swiftly.

"I've had more than enough rest," Robbie responded. "How about it, Mark; up for some good cooking?"

"If I'm not intruding," he said.

Of course you're intruding, I thought, channeling my inner Nurse Ratched. Why don't you just leave while you still have one good leg to hobble out on?

"Of course not!" said Mother, piercing through my troubled thoughts. "Genie, why don't you give Mark a hand."

I'll lend him a hand from the top of the staircase, I thought, as I helped him into the elevator. On the way down to the ground floor, I realized that I was now trying to quiet my inner Bette Davis.

I sat in the very back of the van on the way home, so that Robbie and Mark could be more comfortable in the middle seat. They continued talking about their interests and classes and other things that made it impossible to be part of the conversation. It's just lunch, I kept thinking. Bide your time and play along nicely, before Joan Crawford shows up.

Mother and Dad's fussing over Mark during lunch was difficult, especially when Mother remarked how cute "the walking wounded" looked together. Nor was I all too pleased when I had to help clean up while Robbie and Mark went to hang out in the living room until Mother could drive Mark home. What could they possibly have to talk about all this time?

After cleaning up, Mother insisted that Robbie go rest

while he and I drove Mark home. Robbie again gave Mark the "call me" finger sign as we walked out the door, and Mark obnoxiously responded, "Tonight!"

On the ride to his home, Mother did most of the talking with Mark. After we had dropped him off, Mother asked, "You don't like Mark very much, do you, Genie?"

"Oh! He's OK, I guess. We just don't have that much in common," I responded rather unconvincingly.

"I'm not so sure," Mother said coyly. "I'm not so sure."

We drove most of the way home in silence. I was totally confused by all the feelings swirling inside me, and I think Mother was just trying to find the right words to help. Finally as we pulled into our driveway, Mother said, "I know that you and Robbie are close, Genie, but it's good to have some friends outside the family too."

"I know," I responded. "But why would he want to be friends with the guy who ruined everything." As if that was the only reason that I was upset.

"Mark didn't ruin anything, Sweetie. It was an accident. You might just as well be mad at the ground for hurting both of them. I know it isn't easy. I've been there, but you have to allow Robbie the freedom to choose his own friends. Otherwise, you'll just create a wedge between the two of you and push him further away. I know that you don't want that. And I know that Robbie doesn't want that either."

"I know, but it is so hard sometimes. This guy could ruin everything between Robbie and me."

"He can't ruin what is already there, Sweetie. And he

can't ruin something that isn't. Mark isn't your biggest threat. Your expectation about Robbie is."

"But … if … "

"But and if are ponderous words, Baby. They seldom have anything to do with reality. They sometimes spring out of our imaginations and make us wish for something other than what is clearly in front of us. Robbie's interest in Mark is clearly in front of you. It's OK to want to change things for yourself, but you can't change things for someone else without them wanting it also. Otherwise you run the risk of losing everything. Believe me I know. I've come dangerously close. Do you understand what I'm trying to tell you?"

"So you're saying that I have a big but."

"Yes, Baby. And it's time to lose it or risk making a complete ass out of yourself."

Twenty-One

True to his word, Mark called that night, and every night after that. Heeding Mother's advice, I did my best to stay close to Robbie, and out of their way, despite the fact that more and more of the time that Robbie and I would have spent together was now spent with Mark.

Although they were spending a lot of time together, Robbie seldom mentioned Mark when we spoke. Even at night when he would sit naked on the side of my bed and talk about the day, Mark was absent from the conversation. That was just fine with me, because the last thing I wanted to hear was the name Mark while Robbie was naked.

This kind of "cat and mouse", "waiting for the other shoe to drop" game went on for over a year. Unfortunately, the day finally arrived when I was tagged and my comfort "home free" zone was completely shattered. In other words, the games were finally over.

I was supposed to have a Writing Club meeting that was canceled, and Mother was in the city shopping on that particular day. When I arrived home unexpectedly, Chip stopped me from going upstairs to my room.

"You don't want to go up there right now, Gene," he said.

"Why not?" I asked.

"You just don't, Gene! Believe me!"

I started past him up the stairs as if everything he was saying didn't make sense, because at the time it didn't.

"Gene, don't!" he insisted. "I didn't want to say anything, but they're naked. They're having sex. Robbie and Mark, they're having sex."

"What are you talking about? How do you know that?" I demanded.

"Never mind," he said. "I just do. I wouldn't make something like that up. You'll just embarrass yourself and them if you go up there."

"But that's my room," I said, as if that made any sense, or difference.

"It's his room too, Gene. And you're not supposed to be home for a few more hours."

I just stood there, not knowing what to do. I don't know why it never dawned on me that this would be happening. I guess I wanted to believe that in the end it would be me, not Mark, enjoying what was going on in my room.

"What should I do?" I finally asked.

"Do yourself a favor and go find something, anything to do outside the house," Chip said. "I know that this hurts, but it will hurt a lot more if you see them together right now. Please, Gene! If you want, I'll come with you."

"No! It's OK. Really! It's OK. Thanks, but I think I'd

rather just be alone for awhile, if you don't mind. I'm OK. I just need to, you know, sort things out."

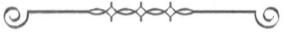

Twenty-Two

I wasn't OK! You can't possibly sort things out when you're out of sorts. I was completely out of my mind with hurt and jealousy when I learned about Robbie and Mark having sex in our room. To hell with all that garbage about waiting for the right person and the right time, I thought. See where that got me! So, if Robbie didn't want me, I was going to find someone who did.

I knew enough about the gay scene in our area to know that there was a place in the park, not too far from where we lived, where gay men often met. I had never been there before, but I was sure as hell going there now. I summoned all my anger and all my courage and stormed over there as quickly as I could.

By the time I got there, the storm had dissipated into little more than hot air. It was a very strange experience, exciting and terrifying at the same time. I wasn't even sure what I was supposed to do or say.

I sat on a bench playing out various scenarios in my

head, none of which were probably realistic. I sat there for about half an hour or so with a few guys passing by, sometimes smiling, but no one stopping to talk. I was pretty scared, so I probably didn't look very receptive. The scenarios weren't working out. I had just about given in to my fears and left, when a good-looking young guy came over and sat down next to me. Naturally, I froze.

"Do you mind if I sit here?" he began. I didn't answer immediately. "If so, you can be honest. I'll just move on if you'd rather be alone." I nodded that it was OK. He smiled. "Nice day!" he continued. "Do you come here often?" I shook my head, No!

He smiled broader. "I thought so. You seem a little shy. I don't mean to be intrusive, but do you mind if I ask how old you are? You seem kind of young and nervous."

"So do you … the young part." I responded as both youth and nerves got the better of me and I got up to leave. "I think I better go."

"Hey! I'm sorry if I offended you. I didn't mean to. I was really just trying to look out for you. You look very young and sweet, kind of innocent, so I wanted to make sure that it was OK for me to … I mean, I was actually kind of hoping that … "

"Me too!" I said, somewhat convincingly, maybe more for myself than for him.

"I don't live far from here. Would you like to come over for a while?"

I actually was on the verge of panicking and saying no, but he was good-looking, probably around nineteen or twenty at most, and I was still upset about Robbie and Mark. So I took a deep breath, steeled myself, and said "Yeah!" and left with him.

On the way to his home, he told me his name was John. I didn't know whether to give my real name or not, so I gave the first name that came to my head, which was Josh. When he mentioned that he just recently had graduated from high school and was nineteen, I lied about being a year behind at eighteen. I didn't know exactly why I was doing this, but I couldn't stop it. I can't even remember what other lies I probably told him along the way, but whatever other information I gave him wasn't true.

John's apartment was a one-room studio in a private home. It was sparsely decorated and looked more like he was moving out than living in. There were only two places to sit, on a small sofa and on the bed. I chose the sofa, but after kicking off his shoes and opening his top shirt, he took my hand and moved me over to the bed. My body trembled.

"I can tell that you're very nervous. Are you going to lie to me, or are you going to admit that you haven't done this much before?" he asked.

"No. I'm not ... I haven't," I stammered. "Done this much before, that is."

"You don't have to be nervous Josh, and you don't have to do anything you don't want to do," he said as he unbuttoned my shirt. "If at any time you become uncomfortable and want to stop, just tell me. It's OK. We'll stop.

Everybody's been there. I just want you to be comfortable and enjoy the experience. OK?"

I nodded that it was.

After finishing with the buttons, he removed my shirt, and gently pushed me back onto the bed. As he started to unbuckle my pants, I became so excited that I was afraid that it would be over before it began. He unzipped my pants, then reached up and gently ran his hands down my chest. His hands moved slowly down to circle the area where he had just unzipped my pants and gently cup and examine my throbbing excitement. He played there awhile, smiling at every shiver and tremor, and then his hands continued down my trouser legs to my feet, where he removed my shoes and socks.

He sensually massaged each foot for a minute or so and then, almost as quickly as a magician removing a tablecloth, he reached up and slid me out of both my pants and briefs.

I was stark naked, on a stranger's bed, and about to have sex, all for the first time in my life. It was all happening so fast, there was no thought, just the fever of excitement. Before I fully understood that this was really happening, every inch of his naked body was pressed firmly against every inch of mine. It felt amazing. He was so warm and soft, and yet very masculine. I surrendered completely as he took control of the situation and whispered for me to just relax.

His hands held both of mine tightly against the sheets as he began to kiss first my lips, then my neck, and then run the warmth of his mouth down and around my entire body. His touch, his mouth, his tongue were all so sensual, so tender, so exciting. He left no part of my body, no digit, no crevice envious of any other part. Everything he did was hypnotically amazing, and every part of my body was throbbing, swirling. I heard my voice sighing, and felt my body jolting and arching as he firmly held me hostage to the ecstasy of my first experience.

My entire body became an erogenous zone under his very able direction. I felt like I was going to either explode from the excitement or combust from the heat. This was so much better than anything I had ever imagined. Like a maestro, he continued building toward and withdrawing from a climax, knowing exactly when to refrain and when to resume the crescendo. Over and over again he teased me with his lips, his tongue, the gentleness of his hands, until my body couldn't take it anymore and erupted much too loudly to the warmth of his mouth and flicker of his tongue.

He never stopped, though. He simply reached up to put his finger to my lips to quiet me, and continued until every bit of energy had been drained from my body into his. Then he crawled up beside me, spooned my limp body in his, kissed the back of my head, and whispered for me to just breathe and relax awhile.

It's impossible to breathe when you've been left breathless, or to relax when you've never been more excited in your life. My brain was replaying every precious second for posterity, so that none of it would ever be lost. I would have been in absolute heaven if I wasn't also plagued with thoughts of what to do next, and when.

All those thoughts were thrown off-track and derailed, however, when John broke the silence and startled me. "Now that we've come this far, if I ask you something, will you be perfectly honest with me?"

I panicked. Without even thinking, I blurted out, "I'm really sorry, I know it was stupid. I was so nervous. My real name is Gene, Gene Poole-Hall, and I'm sixteen, but I'll be seventeen pretty soon."

"OK!" he said with a rather serious smile. "That wasn't what I was going to ask, but it may present a problem. I could get into a lot of trouble if you told anyone that we had sex. I'm not sure that you're above the legal age of consent."

"I wouldn't do that," I swore. "I would never do anything that would hurt you, honest. I won't tell anyone. I'm the one that lied. It's my fault. I never realized that I could get you in trouble. I just wanted it to happen. You have no idea how much this has meant to me. It's just between you and me. It will always be our secret. But does that mean that I can't see you again?"

"Well, actually yes. I'm afraid so," he said rather sadly, "But not for the reason you think. Now it's my turn to confess.

Next week I enter seminary studies. I know that sounds strange after what just happened, but I have been thinking about it for quite awhile, and I think that it's what I'm called to do. It won't be easy, but part of the process is a vow of celibacy. That certainly wouldn't be possible around you.

I didn't know that this, that you, would be this special, this memorable when I saw you. I couldn't stop myself then, and I certainly wouldn't be able to stop myself the next time. You're so beautiful, almost innocently so. You're amazing, really.

I allowed myself to believe everything you said was true, knowing that it probably wasn't, in order to make it all right. Obviously that wasn't right; it was wrong because it wasn't fair to you.

I wasn't thinking very straight either. I guess that I just wanted to break loose one more time, have one more lasting memory.

I'm truly sorry. I hope you understand that I really just wanted to share something special with you, but never at the risk of hurting you. I would like to believe that this wouldn't have happened if I knew that you were underage. But, having said that, I'm truly glad that it did. And though I won't be able to see you again, you will always be far more than I ever imagined possible.

I don't know if I'm making much sense. I'm really trying. Do you understand what I'm trying to say? Are you OK with all this?"

I sat up a little teary eyed, and stared at the kindness in his face. Then, instead of climbing out of bed, I climbed on top of him, as he had earlier done to me and kissed him. I whispered that now it was his turn to relax.

Every touch, every move that he had made earlier, had

been indelibly imprinted in my brain, and I proceeded to repeat each and every one as close to the way he did as possible. He was surprised, but he didn't resist. He just lay back and let me take over.

His body tasted saltier than I might have expected, but then again I didn't really know what to expect. It was actually very pleasing, as was his musk of summer and citrus soap.

As my tongue traveled the course of his body, I took note of his every reaction. When he moaned, I lingered longer, sensing that I may have discovered something on my own. When I had teased enough, I'd move on, only to come back and tease some more. He didn't say a word. He just let me continue until his excitement could continue no longer and he too was spent.

"Would you call that OK?" I asked coyly as I curled back into his spoon.

"The last thing that I would call that is just OK," he responded with a huge grin as he tightened his hold and showered the back of my neck with kisses.

We stayed like that for quite awhile, just enjoying the warmth and feel of each other's bodies. Finally, as I started to get up, I asked, "What was it you were going to ask me before?"

"I almost forgot," he smiled. "You were so nervous, and yet so excited; I was going to ask if that was your first time."

"Well," I said returning his smile, "the second time with you just now was my second time ever."

"I thought so. Usually people with a little more experience don't call on deity more times than a priest at vespers."

"Well, it was kind of a religious experience," I confessed. "It was like I hadn't died and gone to heaven."

"I'm flattered, but, let me ask you, as long as we've gone this far, and all our cards are on the table, would you care to stay awhile longer and maybe even go for a repeat performance?"

"I love encores! I thought you'd never ask," I said nestling back into him.

It's true that the best is always saved for the encore. It was breathtaking. Afterward, we talked extensively about our families, our plans, our favorite this, our least favorite that, and anything that we could think of that would bring us that much closer together and make the experience that much more memorable. Eventually John even suggested a three-peat.

"You're kidding, right?" I said. "A three-peat? You're going to be celibate in a week. I may never see you again. Now's not the time to worry about limitations."

We didn't! And because of that, I stayed way later than I should have.

When I arrived home later that evening, I was so concerned about protecting John that I was able to sound sincere about working on a new school project, and get away with it. I breezed passed my parents, slipped under Robbie's radar while he spoke to Mark on the phone, and would have been home free if I hadn't bumped into Chip on the way to my room. "You look and smell like some virgin bubble that's just been pricked," he laughed. "Let's have the details."

"No!" I whispered as I closed the bedroom door on him.

"I'll haunt you," he threatened through the door.

"You already do," I said. "Now go spook someone else. I need to take a shower."

"You certainly do! And don't forget to gargle, rookie boy. We wouldn't want to leave behind any tell-tale signs or scents, now, would we?" he added as he chased after Dale to break the news.

I knew that Chip and Dale would be haunting me for quite awhile after that night. I didn't realize how much John would be also. No one had ever made me feel the way that he did, physically, emotionally and psychologically. He made me feel that I was the one who was special, that I was the object of desire. He made me feel better about myself than anyone had ever done before, even Robbie.

I still loved Robbie, of course, but now John had carved out an extraordinary place in my life that would always be his, even if I never saw him again. He was not my first love, but he was my first. He cared for me in a way that I thought that Robbie might have, and I loved him for it.

For the first time in my life I began to realize how you can actually romantically love more than one person at the same time. But with John out of the picture, Robbie was the only carrot dangling in front of me. And, though the carrot continued to hold my attention, it too was apparently now way out of my reach.

Normal?

Life goes on, even when there isn't much life in it. I returned to dating my imagination.

Twenty-Three

If there is anything that you can call atypical in our family, it would be a typical Saturday night dinner. The first Saturday in December was such a night. With the exception of Robbie who was out Christmas shopping with Mark in the city, everyone was sitting around the dinner discussing the holidays and all our plans.

The aunts were joking that instead of decorating the trees outside, they would just throw a few lights on their usual Christmas outfits and pose for the neighbors. Mother was already planning Christmas and Hanukkah menus. Aunt Sue was reminding him that Kwanza is also an important holiday, especially to "us Japanegroes." Aunt Allie was feeling a little left out until Mother promised him a Merry Couscous Night. Everyone was laughing and having fun. Then the phone rang.

Mark was calling from Beekman Downtown Hospital. He and Robbie had been attacked by two guys who called them faggots. He remembered that one of them grabbed him from behind. They must have knocked him out. The next thing he remembered, he was waking up in an ambulance on the way to the hospital with a bandage on his head, and Robbie nowhere in sight. He kept asking everyone at the hospital what happened to Robbie, but he never got a straight answer. He was panicked and asked that we please hurry.

Within seconds we were all in the van headed for the hospital. Mother called Beekman on the way, but we arrived while he was still waiting on hold for an answer. In the meantime, Aunt Allie had called his policeman brother, Mohammed, to see if he could be of any help. He promised he would be there shortly.

We pulled in front of the Emergency Room and all filed out, leaving the car right where we stopped. We ran inside and mobbed the front desk so quickly that the intake nurse rushed to find a doctor to pass us off to.

While we were waiting, Mark appeared out of nowhere with the bandage on his head. He was visibly shaken and in tears. He still didn't know anything further and he was sure that he had let Robbie down. He kept crying, "I don't know what happened! I should have been there! I should have been with him! I don't know what happened!"

I was about to throw my arms around him and comfort him, when he dealt this verbal blow that stopped me dead in my tracks. "He's got to be OK," he said. "I love him so much! I should have been with him!"

At first I didn't know what to do. He loves Robbie.

We both obviously love Robbie in much the same way. Mark's advantage was that Robbie obviously loves us differently.

I'm not sure exactly what it was, but something inside of me clicked off the jealousy button, and I rushed to hug Mark. I started rubbing his back the way Robbie would rub mine when I was hurt. It always worked when he did it. "He'll be OK," I said. "We'll all be OK. You'll see."

Mark calmed and started to tell me all that he remembered. I was still hugging him when I looked over his shoulder at the most beautiful sight I have ever seen. Walking out of the Emergency Room door was Robbie, his bad arm in a sling, but otherwise not looking any the worse for wear. He smiled when he saw us all.

Mark, who hadn't seen Robbie yet, had just gotten to the point in his story where he was knocked out when Robbie, so that only I could see, put his index finger to his lips, winked, and then made a fainting gesture with the back of his hand to his forehead.

I understood that it was just between us, but I couldn't help but laugh at our little secret. Mark was shocked at the laugh.

"What?" he cried sadly as though I was trying to hurt or belittle him in some way.

"Christmas!" I said, as I spun him around toward Robbie. "Christmas!"

Mark rushed into Robbie's good arm. They hugged and kissed as tears swelled in all our eyes. Then they both turned and instantaneously waved me into their embrace.

They both kissed me. "Now the circle is complete," Mark added. It was extremely sweet and caring of him. "Christmas!" I thought, "Christmas!"

The rest of the family who had been watching the interaction from across the room rushed into the circle as if Robbie had just won the game. I think in our hearts, he had. When the jumping and cheering had stopped, Mother asked Robbie to fill in all the blanks.

Robbie explained that he and Mark had been taking a shortcut through a parking lot on their way to the New Jersey Path train when two guys came up from behind them and shouted, "Are you guys faggots?"

"I prefer smarter and better dressed than you," Robbie responded, "but that may somehow translate into faggot in Neanderthal."

"At that point one of them grabbed Mark from behind," he said with a slight wink in my direction, "and must have knocked him out. I flashed on the clog episode with the twins and the bullies, and since we had just bought Chip a new pair of wooden heeled clogs, I put the gift to good use. Sorry, Chip! I still owe you an unused gift. I actually hurt my arm swinging the clogs. Great weapon!

Anyway, there were apparently witnesses to the attack who called the police. Our attackers, who are apparently new police recruits, claimed that Mark and I had actually started the whole thing and attacked them first. Since Mark was unconscious, and they were the ones who were hurt and on the ground, the police handcuffed me and brought me here for treatment and questioning. That's why it took so long for me to get out here. They were still questioning me."

Robbie appeared pretty calm about the ordeal, but a flame had been lit in the fireworks factory and Mother was about to explode. "Where are the idiots who hand-cuffed my baby?" he shouted. "Tom, call our lawyer. Al-lie, call your brother. Somebody, call a doctor, because if I get to any of those idiots first they're going to need one. "

Just then a police sergeant appeared. "Calm down everyone," he said. "Let's not get too excited. It's all apparently just a misunderstanding."

"Misunderstanding? What part of hate crime do you not understand?" Mother demanded. "What part of assault and battery did they forget to teach you? Did they make you trade in brain cells for jail cells?"

You could feel the sergeant shrinking as Mother fired shots all around him. "Exactly what type of force are you recruiting that you are protecting these little Nazis?"

"Actually," said Uncle Josh, "I believe that I can help clear things up for the good sergeant, Benji.

Mrs. Rosen, who happens to be in my congregation, watches out her window overlooking the parking lot all night long. I just spoke with her on my cell phone; she'll collaborate Robbie and Mark's story. Also, I know that Mr. Weinbaum, also in my congregation, owns the drug store next to the parking lot. He has a camera focused on the lot. I can get you the film."

The sergeant excused himself and went into the

rooms where the recruits were being held. While he was gone, Mother asked Uncle Josh if what he said was true.

"Of course!" said Uncle Josh. "I wouldn't lie. Mrs. Rosen is always a little tipsy, and will testify to anything that you ask her, whether she has seen it or not. I never said that she was reliable. And Mr. Weinbaum has a camera on his store that hasn't worked for years, but it still has film. I just told the good sergeant that I would get him the film. I never said there was anything on it."

"You would have made a good Catholic," Mother laughed.

"I had a good teacher," Uncle Josh responded.

When the sergeant returned, he looked a little defeated. "Look, they're not bad kids," he tried to explain. "They just had a little too much to drink. They need a bit more polishing. The situation got out of hand too quickly. They never meant to physically hurt the boys, but they panicked when it escalated. There's no sense in ruining their chances for good careers over mistakes we can remedy. I'm sure we can come up with a solution that will make everyone happy. We can send them for sensitivity training."

Mother was not easily being convinced. And while he and the sergeant were jousting, I noticed a nurse visiting the rooms where the two recruits were being held. A short time after the nurse had left, one of the recruits opened his door looking pretty disheveled and beaten. He took one look at Aunt Allie and shouted, "That's the nurse that did this to me. Get her! She karated and judoed me all over the room. She could have killed me!"

"What are you jabbering about? She, or rather he, I apologize, has been here the whole time. Get back in the room while I try to convince these nice people to save your career. Now!" the sergeant shouted.

"Jeez," whispered Aunt Allie with a wink to the rest of us, "You would think that I knew martial arts like my twin brother, Mohammed. Where could that have possibly come from? I hope that the other recruit isn't suffering from the same delusion."

While Mother and the sergeant continued arguing, Robbie conferred with Mark and then pulled Mother into another room. When they re-emerged, Mother said, "OK, this is how it's going to go. Your boys are going through not only sensitivity training, they're also going to volunteer for a few weeks at the Gay and Lesbian Antiviolence Task Force. And you and I will be on hand at the training and at the task force to make sure that it all goes well. Agreed?"

"It sounds fair to me," said the sergeant. "Let me just speak to the boys." When he returned he said, "They've agreed, as long as the killer nurse isn't there, whatever that means."

Mother seemed pleased. "Just remember, if your boys screw up again, policemen or no policemen, they'll be in the ground, not on it."

"Say, you wouldn't be from the Lower Eastside, would you?" the sergeant asked.

"Yeah! Why?

"I think you may be the guy that gave me a well-deserved beating one time for being a bully."

"I remember you," Mother laughed. "You and two other guys. Tom, come quick and say Hi to the guy who beat you up when you were a kid. Josh, remember this guy?"

"Shit!" exclaimed Robbie. "Does Mother know how to throw a reunion or what?"

After a little reminiscing, the sergeant again thanked everyone and told Mother that he would see him again as agreed on.

"You know I'll see you all there," Mother promised and then packed the aunts and Uncle Josh into a cab and the rest of us into the van for a celebratory coming home party. "Christmas!" I thought. "Christmas!"

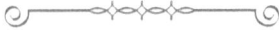

Twenty-Four

The next morning, I was sitting on the side of my bed thinking about the night before when Robbie awoke.

"How are you feeling?" I asked. "Is your arm still sore?"

"A bit," he said, "but why do I get the feeling that I'm not the one who's hurting? What's going on?"

"Nothing," I whispered.

"At the risk of sounding like Mother, I'm good for nothing. Tell me."

"Last night at the hospital, Mark told me that he loved you. I guess I was just wondering if you loved him back."

"Yes," he said, "I'd have to say that I do, though I really haven't admitted that to him yet. Yeah, I do, for a while I guess."

"How come you never said anything to me?" I asked sadly.

Robbie came over and put his good arm around me. "I wanted to, Hot Stuff, for a long time, but I knew that it would hurt you, and I didn't want to do that, not for anything. So, I kept just about everything I could about Mark to myself until I figured out the best way to handle it."

"You knew that it would hurt me?" I asked.

"I broke my arm, not my head, little bro. I'm not deaf, dumb and blond, you know!"

"I would never think of you as dumb," I interjected. "I love you too much. But sometimes you can be pretty blond."

The "I love you part" had slipped out. It was not intentional. It hung in the air for a few seconds, and then I tried to save face by adding, "the only dumb blond thing you ever did was choosing Mark over me," (not really saving face here either.)

Robbie smiled, "I love you too, Hot Stuff, more than you can imagine. You have always been the most important person in my life. I can't even imagine my life without you. I would never choose anyone over you. It's just different with you and Mark. You were just a little kid when we first met. The moment I saw the expression on your face, the aching for family and friends that I had felt all my life disappeared. If I had only found a home for one night, I still would've had that feeling with you. And that was more than I had ever had before.

I promised myself that night that I would do everything in my power not to lose that connection. As beautiful and attractive as you've become, you have always remained my little brother, because that has always been the most precious relationship I've ever had. I would never do anything to ruin that."

"I guess I didn't understand, or didn't want to," I confessed. "I was always so excited by you. I guess that I always wanted more."

"I know," he said. "And there were times that I did too, like the night we were cuddled on the sofa after that altercation with Jimmy and the goons. I had to hide my excitement the same way you tried to hide yours. But I knew that it was important, that it could change things if I didn't. Sex has a way of doing that, of getting in the way.

Can you imagine how upset Mother and Dad would have been if they found out that something had happened between us? Just think how that would have complicated things. I don't think that we could have what we have now if we had done anything.

What we have now, what I hope we will always have, is the most important bond in the world to me. You are the most important person in the world to me."

"I understand," I said. "Somewhere, I guess that I always have. Fantasies aside, I think that I'm just afraid that I'll lose you."

"Oh, Bro! That's what I'm trying to explain to you. You couldn't lose me if you tried. We're a team, we're family, and we're best friends. You'll always be my best Best. So, do you understand? Are we OK?"

"You bet bro!" I smiled as he walked into the shower. But brother, it isn't going to be easy!

Twenty-Five

It wasn't easy, but neither was it as difficult as I thought it would be. Robbie and I still spent a lot of time together. His attitude and affection toward me was completely unchanged by our conversation, much to my relief. He became more comfortable discussing Mark with me, and I in hearing about him.

Mark was kind enough to include me in a lot of things that he and Robbie did, and classy enough to never let me feel like a third wheel. He was beginning to grow on me more than I ever could have imagined. They both sought my help in writing term papers and filling out their college applications. The more time I spent with them, the more I began to realize how good they were for each other.

I loved Robbie, and I wanted nothing but the best for him. If that wasn't me, it sure as hell could be Mark. And I found solace in being the Ben in their Josh and Ruthie story. Those feelings, and a few others that lingered, found their way into another story.

Twenty-Six

LAZARUS RISING

By Gene Poole-Hall

(Age 17)

Sebastian Lazarus was not his uncle. Nor did it appear that he ever would be. His elder namesake was a selfless man, a man loved by many, for many reasons, not the least of which was an ever thoughtful and kind disposition. Time and ingenuity had left the elder Sebastian a wealthy man, but his true wealth was in his heart, and it enriched all that he touched far more than it ever did him. If there was ever a time when the senior Sebastian thought of himself above others, or even thought of himself at all, no one could remember it. The same could not be said of his nephew.

The younger Sebastian had a darkness about him. His thoughts were his own and mirrored little more than his own reflection. After the accidental death of his parents, his uncle's younger brother and wife, the elder Sebastian tried to raise his nephew as though he were his own son, sparing no expense in trying to help the young boy deal with the loss of his parents. He just wanted the boy to be happy, to be more than he had ever allowed himself to be. But the more he tried, the more trying young Sebastian became.

Perhaps his uncle had gone too far by spoiling the boy. Perhaps he had not gone far enough. He loved young Sebastian; the boy was the sun and the moon in the older man's eyes. But, just as the astronomy of family life is not always written in the stars, young Sebastian was not the star that his uncle was. In fact, he was more like a financial and emotional black hole, draining all around him. His appetite was immense. The more he got, the more he wanted. The more he wanted, the more he got. Who his uncle was, and all his uncle had, would one day be his. But he never wanted who his uncle was, he only wanted what his uncle had.

And now, as the younger man turned twenty, all that he wanted was near at hand. A debilitating stroke had left the older man without the ability to move or communicate. In this helpless state, his fate was no longer under his control. His nephew, armed with the power of attorney, was now in control of his uncle and everything his uncle owned. The sole exception was a mysterious ring that he had always coveted and that his uncle never took off. And soon that would be his too.

In the meantime, the paralyzed old man was shipped

Stephen J. Mulrooney

off to a nursing home for whatever care could be given him in whatever time he had left, and his nephew continued to enjoy all that soon would be his. He had no plans to visit his uncle. Why would he? Outside of their name and blood relation, the one thing the two men had in common is that both were gay. And even there, the younger man had his senior trumped. While the younger Sebastian had already enjoyed many relationships, the senior Sebastian, a victim of fear from the prohibitive times of his youth, and later a casualty of the responsibility to raise his nephew, had none to speak of. Not that he could have spoken of them anyway.

The prison of one's own body is a difficult place to live. Yet, in the weeks that passed since his stroke, the senior Sebastian found peace within his circumstances. Without the abilities of speech or movement, it took some adjustment to overcome the loneliness and frustration of just being. He was acutely aware of all that was happening to and around him, though he was alone in this awareness, so the extent of his being was a secret that only he shared. And though he sometimes felt less than human, he was never treated as such. In fact, he was treated rather well by all the staff, and especially by Rick.

Rick was the handsome young nursing assistant who fed, bathed, and clothed him. Rick's voice was so kind and caring, his touch so thoughtful and gentle. It was Rick who told him jokes or stories, even without knowing if they were understood, and who mildly flirted with him without ever knowing how much it was appreciated. It

was Rick who constantly encouraged him not to be discouraged, to find courage in his present situation. Rick
knew that someone was at home in that body. Even if he
couldn't answer the door, Rick was still going to visit.

Sebastian felt that, if he had only met this young man
fifty years ago, things would be different and he would
woo him. Then again, he had never wooed anyone, so how
could he be sure. If there was any fault in Rick, it was that
Rick reminded Sebastian of all that might have been, perhaps even what should have been, but now would never
be.

How Sebastian wished that he could speak with Rick,
tell him how much his visits meant to him, and perhaps
even return a flirt or two. If only he could feel Rick's hands
on his body as he bathed and dressed him. If only …

While the older Sebastian was busy working at finding
peace, the younger one was busy being a piece of work.
His days were an ocean of self-indulgence, and his nights
teemed with a sea of men. His debauchery and ignorance
of his uncle's situation would have continued unimpeded
had not yet another selfish thought swept through his
mind. The ring. He almost forgot all about the ring. Surely
his uncle had no use for it now. The old man would probably never even know that it was gone. And who knows,
someone else may take it in the meantime. Yes, taking the
ring now was definitely the right thing to do. And so he
decided he would.

The older Sebastian was thrilled to see his nephew
when he entered his room, although he had no way of let-

ting him know. Not knowing how much his uncle understood, the young man probably would have made no pretense of his mission had Rick not entered the room to take care of his patient. But the younger Sebastian was skilled in the charms of pretense, and within a short time Rick had been charmed.

Rick's infatuation with Sebastian was evident from the beginning. The nephew soaked in the attention while feigning concern for his uncle and interest in Rick's stories of how he enjoyed caring for him. All the while, a profound sadness swelled in the older Sebastian as he watched the interaction. He knew that, given the chance, his nephew would surely hurt this beautiful young man. And Rick deserved so much more. He deserved someone who could truly love him, be a partner to him, someone who would do everything possible to make him happy. He deserves someone like me, the older man thought. Well, at least me when I was younger.

Rick stayed and mildly flirted far longer than he should have. When he finally realized how long he had dallied, he awkwardly asked the young Sebastian if they might get together again soon, perhaps over coffee, and continue their conversation. He quickly wrote down his phone number and backed out of the room, blushing and smiling all the way. Young Sebastian smiled and put the number in his pocket, whispering at his uncle, "Perhaps if he were a doctor. Perhaps."

Perhaps if you were a better person, his uncle thought, relieved at his nephew's apparent disinterest in Rick, or perhaps if you cared for anything but yourself. And then as a wave of guilt swept in, he thought, perhaps if I had done a better job of raising you. Perhaps, if we had spoken more, if I had told you of my failures, my fears, my loneliness, or perhaps if I had listened more, listened to your fears, your failures, your loneliness, things would be different. But they are not. And what good do these thoughts do us now, my child, what good?

I wanted so much for you that I forgot to ask what you wanted for yourself. Did I fail you? Had I allowed you to share more of yourself then, would you be able to share more of it now? For my part, please forgive me, and know somehow that I always love you, and all that diminishes you for whatever reason, diminishes me also.

Of course young Sebastian knew none of these thoughts. Besides, he was too busy soaping the old man's finger to get the ring, having already failed at prying it off. Just a little bit more and … Yes!

Although he could not feel the ring leave his finger for the first time in memory, a strange sensation passed over the old man as it did, and he closed his eyes to fathom it. At the same time, his nephew slipped the prize onto his finger. And he too closed his eyes to feel its power, to feel his victory.

How strange it was. When the young man opened his eyes, he could see himself standing in front of himself. What a strange vision this is, he thought. He looked so real, standing there in front of himself, eyes still closed as though still taking in the moment. Such a strange dream, he thought. He went to say something, but could not find his voice. He went to touch this vision, but could not move a muscle. And as he struggled to come to terms with what was happening, he watched as the vision opened his eyes, examined himself in disbelief, and moved around the floor. And then it spoke. "Thank you, nephew," the vision said, "Someday, when we are both ready, I will repay you. Till then, know that I love you." Smiling, he quickly disappeared out the door.

It took awhile for the horror to set in. After all, this was impossible. Wasn't it? Was he really trapped in the old man's body? Wasn't he somehow only dreaming this? For hours he tried to wake from his predicament, only to realize more and more that he was fully awake. How could the old man do this to him? This was a trap. His uncle had to know this would happen. Why didn't he warn him? These thoughts played over and over in his mind until they were interrupted by Rick entering the room.

"Guess what, old buddy," Rick said, smiling ear to ear. "Your nephew called me a little while ago and we are going to get together for coffee. He's amazing! He sounded even sweeter than he did before. I wasn't sure if he liked me as much as I liked him before he called, but he sounded so excited on the phone. This could be good. I think this may work out. I'll keep you posted." And again backing out of the door, this time flushed with excitement, he added, "And don't worry. I didn't forget. I'll be back in a little while for your bath."

"What is he kidding?" Sebastian thought. "Does he really think I'm worried about a bath when my uncle is running around somewhere with my body. Who knows what he is going to do with it."

He truly wanted to hate his uncle for leaving him like he did, but somehow in his idleness, thoughts of his own behavior kept creeping in to modify his feelings. There are two sides to every story, but there are many stories to each side. The shadows of his uncle's stories still remained within his body. Sebastian could feel them. With nothing else to do or feel, he began to explore them. He felt their loneliness, a loneliness far older than his uncle's stroke. He felt his uncle's craving for a natural return of affection. He felt the older man's love for him that was never demonstratively returned. He felt his uncle's frustration at trying to get through his nephew's pain and anger over the death of his parents. He felt his uncle's failure. For the first time in a long time he felt a tremendous urge to cry, to cry for his uncle, to cry for himself, but even this was denied him by this body.

Maybe I wasn't the nicest person in the world, he thought, maybe I was a little too self-centered sometimes, but I don't deserve this. No one deserved this. And then it hit him. No one deserved this, not even his uncle, especially not his uncle. The only one he ever really hurt was himself. Sebastian had plenty of time to ponder this, and he pondered this plenty.

His thoughts were interrupted by Rick who apologized for being late for Sebastian's bath. Rick had apparently met the older, or rather now younger, Sebastian for coffee during his break and was gushing about how they were going to meet again tomorrow on his day off and spend the entire day together. Oh good! Sebastian thought. My uncle is going on my date with this guy and my body, and I get to hear about it. Does it get any better than this?

It did. He got to meet Rick on a very different level, and he found himself leveled in more ways than one. "I have a surprise for you," Rick said as he gently lifted Sebastian across the room and propped him in the shower. "Now don't get frisky," he warned with a wink. "We both know how you can be." Then as he carefully removed Sebastian's bedclothes and made sure the water temperature was perfect, he whispered, "Now don't tell anyone. I can tell how much you like this. I can sometimes hear what you can't say. But I'd be in trouble if they found out, so it's our secret. You're only allowed a sponge bath."

Rick gently bathed Sebastian, dried him, clothed him, combed his hair, brushed his teeth and carried him carefully back to bed, all the while humming something so off-key that Sebastian had no idea what it could be. After tucking him in, Rick brushed Sebastian's hair with his fingers and said, "I bet you could have stolen my heart when you were younger, just the way your nephew is starting to do. Somehow I know that you two are very much alike. Chips off some high-class block, I think. Maybe someday I'll have as good a relationship with him as I have with you. Who knows! Maybe I'll even get to give him a shower, or rather shower with him, or ..." Rick realized he was prattling. "Never mind," he blushed. "So what do you think?

If we make it to the shower, should I hold back on the singing?"

After Rick left, Sebastian was taken by the young man's gentleness, compassion and understanding. He began to wonder what it would have been like to feel this gentle soul's hands on his body as he bathed him, to feel Rick slip his clothes off and on, and then to feel him caress his hair as he spoke. He wondered if his uncle ever had those thoughts. Is he having them now, now that he has the opportunity, now that he's free? Will his uncle finally experience what he longed to experience for so long. For the first time, the nephew hoped so. He hoped that his body might help to dissipate some of his uncle's lingering shadows. He began to realize that for the first time in a long time he actually cared for someone other than himself. Perhaps somewhere deep inside, he had wanted to care all along. He fell asleep dreaming about Rick and his uncle, dreaming about Rick and him, and in some small way he fell asleep happy.

Two days later, Rick was there in his room bright and early, eager to tell Sebastian about his date. He told Sebastian about how much fun they had just talking and walking around the city for most of the afternoon. He told him how he took his nephew home and made him dinner. How they laughed and played while cleaning the dishes and straightening the table. How they listened to music on the sofa and eventually slipped into each other's arms. And finally, he related how he talked the younger Sebastian into spending the night, such a glorious night.

Rick was surprisingly comfortable as he described their love-making as the most beautiful experience of his life, and he confessed his surprise at how innocent and inexperienced Sebastian seemed. Quite different he said from the impression of their initial meeting. He told the old man that there were tears in the young Sebastian's eyes as he whispered his happiness. How Sebastian couldn't contain them any longer as he related that he had waited all his life for something so beautiful to happen. Strange thoughts from such a young man, Rick had thought. Yet Sebastian repeated them over and over again the second and third time.

"Your nephew said that it would be OK to tell you all this," Rick told the old man. "And I know that you couldn't stop me if I went too far. But I had to share this with you. I feel that you are somehow responsible for us meeting, responsible for us getting together, and responsible for something wonderfully breathtaking. And I just had to tell you, to thank you. To let you know that, despite the unfairness of your illness, you are still a part of wondrous things. Forgive me if it was wrong of me to go this far. I cannot help but think it wasn't. And I'm going to high five you if I'm right." With that, he raised Sebastian's hand up, gave him a high five, and gently kissed him thank you on his cheek. "See, I knew that I was right," he smiled as he left.

Over the next few days, Rick continued to tell Sebastian about the dates and conversations he had with his uncle, or rather nephew. And while doing so, he continued to provide care so lovingly to the older man that Sebastian also found himself falling deeper and deeper in love with this man. How foolish I have been, he thought, as he listened and received such tender care. I am actually happy for my uncle. He and Rick deserve each other. I only wish that there had been more of my uncle and less of me in that body before it was no longer mine.

As though sensing every thought, the now younger Sebastian, looking radiantly happy, walked into the room. "This body was never anything but yours, my son," he said kissing his nephew's forehead. "As it was before, all that I have is yours and will be returned to you. We both had so much to learn. And I thank my father, your grandfather, for giving us this family ring to guide us. How it works I do not know. But evidently it does, and that is all that matters." He knelt down in front of his old body, and as the tears came to his eyes he whispered, "Rick is a wonderful man. I doubt that anyone could do better. But it is your life. You must decide for yourself, but I hope that you will give him a chance. You both deserve it." And with that he kissed the old man on the cheek, slipped the ring back on the old man's finger and gently slipped back into his old body.

The younger Sebastian didn't even realize that his eyes had been closed when he opened them and found himself back in his own body. He laughed and danced and spun around in circles before running over to his uncle and kissing him. "You will never regret anything you did for me, uncle. I promise. I will make you proud of me yet. Perhaps I'll even make me proud of me yet. And as for Rick, I want so much for it to work. I can't be you, but I hope to make him fall in love with that part of me that I want to be just like you. Maybe that will be enough. I have a plan, and I'll explain more later when I have it all worked out. In the meantime, I will visit you tomorrow, and tomorrow, and as long as there are tomorrows. You will not be lonely in there anymore, Uncle. I promise."

The next day, young Sebastian appeared bright and early as promised. "OK, Uncle," he said. "This is how it plays out. I have a date for the movies with Rick tomorrow and again for a baseball game on Friday. I am trying to be more like you, but I'm not ready for a baseball game," he smiled with a wink. On Friday, I get the ring and you get the game. And uncle, don't wear him out. I have another date on Saturday." He gently ran his fingers through his uncle's hair. "I hope that someday Rick feels the same way about me as me as he does about you as me. Boy! That must be the weirdest sentence I'll ever speak. But until that day, Uncle, I think that a tag team arrangement will work to all our advantage. What do you say, partner? Are you up to the challenge?"

Tears started streaming from the old man's eyes. They both knew from experience that he hadn't been able to do so since the stroke. "See that, Uncle", the younger man said as tears also started streaming from his eyes, "at the risk of sounding like an old movie, I think that this is the beginning of a beautiful friendship."

Twenty-Seven

Mark and Robbie both decided to attend Rutgers University in New Jersey. Mark's parents had some influence at the university, which I think gave Robbie that little extra boost he needed for admission. His parents had apparently grown quite fond of Robbie, and accepted their relationship, to the point that they even helped them set up room together in the university's dorms.

I was lost without Robbie in my room. Although we talked every day, and he would come home every other weekend, the hole in my life was too huge to fill. I became sullen and aloof. I kept to myself and continued to write, but my writing became much darker, reflective of a loss that I couldn't grapple with. It was only when Robbie was home that the remnants of my personality would emerge, only to dissipate again soon after he left.

Chip and Dale were more than wonderful in trying to bring me out of my funk. Mother and Dad did their best also, but with little success. Even the visits of Uncle Josh and the aunts did little to lighten my mood. I was being a baby, and I knew it, but the hole was still there inside me, and I couldn't seem to fill it.

On the night of my eighteenth birthday, everyone gathered to help me celebrate. I was trying to be upbeat and not lick my wounds, when Robbie and Mark arrived with a salve. They brought me a computer with an attachment that allowed me to see and talk to them every night. It was just what the baby doctor ordered. My bedroom didn't seem as lonely as I watched them hustling and bustling around theirs each night. And each night I got to shut down with a "Goodnight, Hot Stuff!" It was all that I needed. The "terrible" before my teens was fading.

With my mood lightened, I was able to turn my focus on college applications. I thought about applying to Rutgers, and was even encouraged to do so by Robbie and Mark, but I knew that it was time to cut the cord. I wasn't sure that I was ready to abandon the nest yet, so I set my sights on Columbia University, a great choice with a good commute.

Uncle Josh managed to procure a few impressive letters of recommendation, and with my grades, I was in. It was so unbelievable. I was beginning to feel like an adult. In a few months Mother and Dad could proudly say, "My son, who goes to Columbia."

Twenty-Eight

That summer actually began without any vacation plans. Robbie and Mark both had taken summer jobs to help with tuition, I was looking for one to help pay for the high cost of tuition at Columbia, and the twins began exploring college options of their own. The summer was in a state of flux when Robbie showed up unexpectedly at dinner one evening with news that would shake and shape everything.

He and Mark had decided to get married. Marriage between same sex couples was now legal in New York, and even though they knew that they were still young, politically and romantically, they knew it was the right thing for them to do. They were in love and couldn't imagine not spending their lives together, so why not let the world know how they felt.

"Hot Stuff! I'm really sorry that I didn't break the news to you first in private," he said. "You deserve that. But it's all so new, and you were all together, so … Anyway, I hope that you'll forgive me and be my best man.

"I love you, Robbie! Of course, I'd be honored," I answered somewhat shocked, but sincere.

"There's more," he said. "We were thinking of getting married in August on Mother and Dad's anniversary. Mark and I were wondering if my parents wouldn't mind legitimizing me a little more by joining in a double ceremony. It would be so cool to see you two finally get hitched, and I'm sure that seeing you two exchange vows after all these years would mean as much to all of us as it will to you. Soooo … Dad? … Mother?"

"I love you Ben," Dad said. "It's always been you! How about we legitimize all these bastards?"

"You're such a romantic," Mother laughed. "We're in!"

And so the summer plans began.

Twenty-Nine

I wasn't able to find more than a part-time summer job that summer, but with scholarships and a little support from my parents, I knew that I would make it. Besides it gave me more time to help out with the weddings. Not that it was needed with the aunts mixed in the fray.

Mark's parents procured the hall in a country club that they belonged to in upstate New York. The aunts placed themselves in charge of food and decorations. Robbie and Mother asked Uncle Josh to officiate at the wedding, which he of course agreed to do. Chip and Dale were put in charge of "appropriate" music. And I was responsible for certificates, licenses, tuxedo rentals, and anything else that would make the grooms' lives a bit less chaotic. With this group, that was harder than it sounds.

All went fairly well, and August rolled around much too quickly before I realized that there was something that I had not even thought of. It happened at dinner, less than a week before the wedding when Chip and Dale mentioned the dates they were bringing to the wedding. They had dates. Everyone in the immediate family had dates. If I was going to have a date, it was going to be either Aunt Sue or Aunt Allie.

I wondered how Uncle Josh felt about a date.

Thirty

I f there is anything more difficult than watching the love of your life officially become the love of someone else's life, it's doing it alone.

It had been over a year since the day that I met John. And the day had remained so special that it hadn't been repeated with anyone since. I knew that I was extremely fortunate the first time, and I wanted the next to be just as precious, only this time to last for more than one day. It didn't happen, so I was dateless for the two most impor tant weddings outside of my own that I would ever attend.

Mother and Dad's and Robbie and Mark's joint wedding ceremony was held in the same hall as the reception. Aunt Sue and Aunt Allie had spent the entire morning and afternoon beautifully decorating it with flowers, and ribbons, and sashes, so that it looked more like a room in some princely palace than a catering hall. The twins set up a great sound system and arranged an excellent mixture of soft rock and show tunes that anyone would find both touching and pleasing. Uncle Josh spent the day preparing a civil ceremony for officiating his first same sex double wedding. And I spent the day helping all the grooms prepare for their big day, and preparing myself for double best man duties.

The hall was packed with Mark and Robbie's friends, extended families from both sides, and more than a handful of Mother and Dad's friends. Everyone seemed impressed by the decorations, and they were visibly excited by the uniqueness of the event. As this was a civil ceremony, Uncle Josh entered the hall in a suit, and looked more like a minister than a rabbi. Mark's mother and I were the witnesses for Mark and Robbie's wedding, and Robbie and I were the witnesses for our parents.

The ceremony was more than beautiful. Everyone, including Uncle Josh while performing the ceremony, had tears in their eyes. None of the participants had ever looked as happy or more beautiful in their lives. That was especially the case for Mother, who married one great love in his life while being married by the other. I even managed to get caught up in the tidal wave of their happiness, despite being solo and losing Robbie.

At the conclusion of the ceremony, the aunts made sure that the hall rained a sea of rainbow-colored confetti and balloons as the twins blasted "Joy to the World," by Three Dog Night over the sound system. As the celebration began, my only-ness began to sink in deeper as couples and friends began to pair off all around the room. I searched the hall trying to find a table or corner where I would feel less obtrusive. As I was slipping across the dance floor toward the table where Uncle Josh was sitting, I felt a hand on my shoulder. I turned to find this stunningly handsome Asian guy who introduced himself as one of Mark's friends.

His name was Bryan, and he looked and dressed like some gorgeous model or film star. A few years earlier, and I'm sure that my jaw would have dropped a la Robbie. He said that he had been watching me for a while, and it appeared that I, like he, had arrived stag, and that we should probably do something about it. I was too flattered to do more than smile and agree. He asked me to wait a few minutes while he made apologies to a few friends that he was with. He promised to catch up with me as soon as possible. I was thrilled.

After about twenty minutes or so Bryan returned grinning and said, "You must be a pretty special young man. Robbie, Mark, and one of your fathers have already warned me to be very good to you and not hurt you, or I would have to answer to them."

Embarrassed, I apologized and explained that my family, which now included Mark, tends to be a little overprotective. "You can probably expect a visit from both Chip and Dale shortly," I added apologetically.

"Do you want to know the most amazing thing?" he whispered in my ear with a breath that was so hot and sexy that I almost melted right on the dance floor. "I am going to be good to you, and I am going hurt you, and it's all going to happen in just a little while. Only none of it's going to be in the way that they're afraid of."

"I don't under …" I started to say as he put his finger to my lips.

"Shhh!" he sizzled inside my ear. "Just follow me."

"I can't," I started to protest. "The wedding … my family … "

"Everyone is having fun." His hot breath whispered further melting my resolve. "It's our turn. Come on! Don't be such a baby. You want to have a good time, don't you? Well! I'm a real good time. Now come on!"

I followed him down a back set of stairs to a bathroom far from all the activity. Once inside, he spun me around, pushed me face first against a wall and unbuckled and dropped his pants and mine. Then, he reached around and grabbed hold of me from behind with both his hands and pressed himself up against me. The heat and moistness of his lips sent shivers down my spine and buckled my knees as he described what he was about to do to me, and I could feel the firmness of his excitement rubbing against me as he began to stroke at mine.

"I've never done this," I protested.

"You're just trying to get me hotter." His words burned in my ear.

"No! Seriously …. "

"Now's your time, Baby," he whispered. "Yours, and mine … seriously!"

"It really hurts, Bryan."

"I warned you that I would hurt you," he whispered as he stroked and slowly entered me at the same time.

"Bryan, don't!" I yelled much too loud. The pain was so great that I wanted to scream even louder, but I knew that

I couldn't. "Please stop." I tried to pull away, but he had me pinned against the wall.

He bit down hard on my neck as he pressed all the way inside me. I thought that I would pass out as my body trembled in reaction. He kept whispering how good it felt as he held still for awhile, still stroking me.

As he started to pump inside me, the pain brought tears to my eyes. "Bryan, please!"

"Say it again," was all he would respond.

"Please!"

"That's exactly what I'm going to do, Baby … please you and please me."

His hot breath kept whispering things in my ear that I would never repeat. He graphically described what he was doing to me, what else he was going to do, and how much I was going to love it. I stopped struggling. I'm not even sure why. I think that my resolve was weakened by the hotness of his breath and the excitement of the way that he completely took control of my body.

"You are mine now," he whispered as he nibbled at my ear and again bit my neck. "Soon you'll be begging me to do this. The more you think about it, the more you are going to want it."

And then, as he continued thrusting and stroking me he added, "Tell me how much you want it, Gene. Tell me!"

I wanted him to stop and never wanted him to stop at the same time. The pain eventually gave way to an excitement I hadn't known before, and I relaxed into the pleasure of surrender, telling him exactly what he wanted to hear, until his orgasm inside me and mine outside exploded at the same time.

It was more than mind-blowing. I felt as if I was in some altered state, and for that time I truly was his. He remained inside me awhile longer saying, "I want you to get used to this, Gene. I want to hear you ask for it, and I want to hear you say how much you want it when you do."

If I had a little more self-respect at the time, I might have thought of something clever to say. Instead, I just nodded my head in agreement, and let him help me clean up and return to the party.

Now, if there is one thing everyone knows about sex, it's that everyone knows when you've just had it. We re-entered the hall to stares and looks of wonder and concern, and you could tell we were missed.

We separated to rejoin our friends and family who didn't say anything, I glanced over at Bryan, who seemed to revel in the attention of the assumptions. I even caught him giving a couple of high fives. I started to shrink from the embarrassment of what I had just done at my parents' and brother's weddings.

"He'll be giving a couple of low fives with the casts on his arms," Dale startled me from behind. "This better not be some one-shot conquest," she added, embarrassing me further.

"He's pretty hot!" Chip responded. "He can conquer me anytime."

"You're a mental slut," she countered. "Gene has class, or at least he used to."

I was crawling even further into a hole when Robbie and Mark pulled me away.

"Are you OK?" Robbie asked, truly concerned.

"Did he do anything to hurt you?" Mark countered. "I'll throw him out on his ear if he hurt you."

"I'm OK! Really!" I tried to assure them, unaware of the telltale marks on my neck. "It was nothing. He was just being flirtatious."

"Bryan's a player," Mark warned. "I should never have let him near you."

I was about to try to defend myself as responsible enough to know what I was doing when Bryan walked over, reached into my pocket, pulled out my cell phone, and dialed his number.

"Now that I have your number, I'll call you tomorrow, and we'll do something. It was great talking to you. In the meantime, come on over and let me introduce you to my friends."

As Bryan pulled me away, I felt like he helped me save face a bit. If I had to wear a scarlet letter, I'd rather it be an A than a P for pathetic.

As we left, I overheard Mark say, "Well, that may be a positive sign. I guess that if anyone can change a leopard's spots, Gene can."

"I hope so," Robbie added, still within hearing distance. "If he can't, you can be damn sure that I will, one way or another."

My heart smiled as I walked away.

Thirty-One

There has never been a spot remover that could change a leopard's spots. Bryan called me the next morning and asked if I had thought about what we had done at the reception. I confessed that I had. He was extremely pleased, and started recounting what he had done to me in the bathroom and how good it felt to do it. He told me how hot thinking about it made him, and what else he was planning to do to me, and how good it was going to feel. He described everything in such hot and vivid detail that his voice and words whipped me into an excited frenzy. And when he asked me to beg for it, I couldn't believe it. I did.

A short time later, he drove over to my house, thrust me into the backseat of his car, and in the same excited frenzy that drove me crazy on the phone, took me right there in our driveway. It was very quick, and very exciting. And then, as quickly as he came, he left.

After it was over, I couldn't believe what I had done

right outside my own home. It wasn't even "what was I thinking?" because I certainly wasn't doing any thinking at all. I returned to my room, prayed that no one had seen me, and tried not to admit how excited I still felt in spite of how embarrassing the whole situation was.

I felt I was losing it. What I didn't understand at the time was that I had already lost it. Bryan apparently had me in more ways than one. I had become his possession, and he became my obsession. Somehow, that gave him ten-tenths of the law.

Over the next few weeks, as my obsession with him grew, I was a passive participant in many of Bryan's sexual fantasies as he took possession of my body and had me whenever and wherever he wanted. He had me in the movie theater, he had me on the beach, he had me in the park, and he had me wherever he felt like parking. I had become someone else, not me, just his. I had become a recessive Gene.

It took me weeks to realize that Bryan never did anything with me except have sex. With the exception of the movie theater, where we had sex, we didn't go anywhere, see anyone, hang out with friends, or do anything else. I was less than a cheap date because there was never a date. That only left me with cheap.

When I asked him about it, Bryan just laughed and said, "Do you want to do something special? Meet me in the city in front of the Museum of Natural History, and we'll do something special."

By the time I got there it was already dark and the museum was closed. Bryan told me not to worry; we were still going to do something special. We took a shortcut through Central Park, and when we got to a dark heavily wooded area, he stopped and told me to take off all my clothes.

"Bryan, you promised," I protested.

"I know," he said, "but first I get to do something special." Then he opened my pants and took hold of me as he had done so many times before.

"But it's dangerous. We might get caught."

"The only thing you're going to get caught on is me," he boasted. "Now take everything off."

"But why everything?"

"Because I want you to! Isn't that enough?"

And that other person, who was no longer me, did exactly what Bryan wanted him to without further question.

Sex with Bryan had always been hot and exciting. That was part of the obsession. Sex when you're cold and terrified, however, is neither, but my lack of active participation didn't seem to bother Bryan as long as he could have a good time. After he finished, I tried to gather my clothes in the dark. We heard someone approaching and saw a flashlight heading straight toward us.

"Bryan, help me find my clothes," I whispered as I found my shirt and slipped into it.

No answer.

"Bryan, where are you?" as I gathered my shoes and socks.

Still no answer.

All of a sudden the flashlight attached to a policeman shined upon me. "What are you doing here in the dark like that?" he demanded.

"I'm sorry! I had to go to the bathroom and I couldn't wait," I lied.

"So you took off all your clothes?"

"I didn't want to get anything on them. It was kind of an emergency."

"Who was that with you?"

"A friend, but he got scared when we heard someone coming. We didn't know you were a policeman."

"Let me see some ID," he demanded.

I found my pants, pulled out my wallet and gave him all my identification

"OK, get your things and come with me," he said.

"But …"

"Come on!"

He let me get dressed, led me out of the park, and sat me in the back of his car. I was relieved that he hadn't handcuffed me, but I was so afraid and embarrassed about being arrested that I started to cry.

He drove me to some apartment building on the West Side and told me to wait right where I was. He already had all my ID information, so there was no way I was going to do anything but what he said. After a short while, he returned and brought me upstairs to one of the apartments. I was more scared than I had ever been in my life. I couldn't imagine what was going on, or what was going to happen to me.

We stepped into the apartment and a voice from another room said that he was just getting off the phone and would be right there. The officer didn't say anything. He just stared at me and continued to flip through my identification. Minutes seemed like hours.

Finally, the sergeant from the night that Robbie was attacked entered the room. It was both a shock and a relief at the same time.

"Well young man," he said. "I just got off the phone with one of your fathers. He did me a great favor once, and now I'm returning it. You were pretty lucky to be picked up by one of the recruits from the night that we met." The policeman actually smiled and gave a little wave. "You could have been in a bit of trouble had it been anyone else. Fortunately, he remembered the name and recognized you. That's why he brought you here."

"Thank you!" I cried looking at them both with tears streaming down my face. "I wasn't thinking. I swear I'll never get in trouble again."

"Good boy!" The sergeant said. "Now come on. I told Ben that I'd give you a ride home."

The sergeant was really pleasant all the way home. He never asked anything about what happened in the park. There were no scary warnings about what could have happened, or next time. He just reminisced about the "old neighborhood" and how much everything has changed. Then he told me a little secret that he hadn't yet told Mother. One of the recruits, the one who had picked me up, was his nephew. It wasn't always the case, but he was sure that his nephew was going to be a model policeman, in large part because of something Mother had done during sensitivity training.

During the training, Mother, who had taken on an active role in the class, called on the recruit to stand in front of the class for questioning. The sergeant and the recruit became extremely uncomfortable, because they were sure that an embarrassing situation was unfolding. Instead, Mother carefully led the recruit through a series of questions and situations where all the right answers were pretty much self-evident.

When they finished, Mother praised the recruit as being a perfect model for the rest of the class, and said he hoped that they would all become as fine an officer as the sergeant's nephew was going to be. He never forgot the kindness, and he has done his best to become the kind of officer that Mother would be proud of.

"You're very lucky to have a father like that," the sergeant finished. "His compassion and intellect is as big as his heart, which is obviously immense. I hope that for his sake and yours that you too become the type of person he can be proud of."

I sank into even deeper remorse. I had strayed so far that I thought I would never be able to find my way back.

It is said that the greatest pain is that which you can't tell others. How could I explain this to anyone? I couldn't even imagine what Mother and the rest of my family would think of me. I wanted to die. I prayed for it. What I didn't realize at the time was that my prayer had been answered. The part of me that needed to die - did, then and there.

When we got home, Mother told me to go to my room for now, and we would talk in the morning when we had more time to think about what we wanted to say. As I headed upstairs, he said that my father had gone to bed early, and the twins were at a school project sleepover at a friend's house, so for now this was just between us.

I went to my room, and Mother invited the sergeant in for a drink and some further reminiscing. I was relieved not to have to talk about anything that happened, but found myself sobbing most of the night as the embarrassment played over and over again in my mind.

The next morning before I even got out of bed, Bryan called. "You bastard!" I shouted. "You left me."

"Are you all right?" he asked, almost smugly.

"No thanks to you," I tore back.

"Did you get arrested?"

"Again, no thanks to you."

"If I had stayed, you probably would have, so you can thank me."

I did by hanging up the phone just as Mother came to the door. "Who was that?" he asked as he entered the room.

"Nobody!" I said.

"Glad to hear it. That's who I thought it was. Can we talk?"

"Are we going to play chess?" I asked, more earnest than upset.

NORMAL?

"I probably deserve that for not being there for you more when you wanted it," he said. "But you have to understand, Genie, that you've always been my baby. And, although you've probably had a hard time with me always thinking that way, I've had a hard time thinking about you as anything else.

I know that you're a young man now, but I still want to hold you in my arms and rock you to sleep telling lies about your Aunts Sue and Allie. I miss those times, Baby, and I miss you missing them, too.

But you can talk to me. I'm here for you now, no more games. Just cut me this slack, keep the sex parts as generic as possible, and I'll be more best friend than parent. Deal?"

It was a far better deal than I had ever hoped for. And we both did a fairly admirable job of keeping up with our ends of the bargain as I recounted my history with Bryan. By the end, I was back in Mother's arms, in tears, and he was rocking me like old times. There were tears in his eyes too as he consoled me. "It's OK, Baby; we've all been places we shouldn't have gone. Lord knows, I have. What's important is not where you've been, but where you're going."

Then he smiled, "If you keep looking behind you, you're bound to see an ass that you'd rather forget.

Tell you what! I'll let you in on a little secret of mine. It's not a big one, but maybe it will make you smile. Sometimes, when you kids are all in bed, and everything is nice and quiet, your father and I like to watch a video or two to kind of get us in the mood."

"Ewww!" I interrupted.

"Hey! We're in best friend mode, remember! Anyway, when we go away on vacation, I don't want anyone to find them should anything happen to us and have them think that they're mine. So I hide them in your father's underwear drawer, so that when they're found, they'll think that if anyone is a pervert, it's him."

"I did the same thing to Robbie!" I smiled.

"What?"

"Just kidding!"

"Don't play with your Mother's heart, Genie! You're too much a part of it."

"I know, Mother. I'm sorry! It's just that after I lost Robbie … I mean that I always dreamt that Robbie and I would be more, you know?"

"I know, Baby! Not every 'happily ever after' winds up with the prince of your dreams, but that doesn't mean that you can't wind up with a prince who is a dream."

"But all my dreams turn out to be either wet or nightmares!" Then, realizing who I was talking to, I apologized. "Sorry! That just slipped out."

"That's OK, Genie, you're talking to your best friend. You have to remember, Baby, that you're still young. Your life is supposed to be filled with success and failure, dreams and mistakes. That's normal. It's even normal to be the fool that's added to the fire. That's how you learn and grow.

Youth is when you have the energy to do, and be, and experience anything and everything. It's not wasted on the young, but it's easily wasted by them. As you get older, responsibilities make it more and more irresponsible to take as many chances or risks. It becomes more and more difficult to hear the knock of opportunity. Eventually, you lose the impulses that are the core of youth.

Few people look back on their youth and regret the chances they took or the mistakes they made. Most people look back and wish that they had taken and made more."

"Bryan was certainly a mistake I could have done without. He never treated me well. He never allowed me to be myself; for the most part, he just used me. Yet when I was with him, he took my breath away."

"Look, Baby! I'm not going to tell you what to do. You have to decide that on your own. But I will say that maybe there is a reason there is a why in the middle of Bryan's name. And even though he takes your breath away, I'd rather be with someone that lets me breathe than someone who suffocates me. Eventually, he was bound to either put a brake on, or break your heart. Any relationship that doesn't build you up, diminishes you, if only in the waste of time better spent."

"I'm not going to see him again," I said as all the embarrassment from the night before began to pool in my eyes once more. "I never want to be that person again. Is everyone disappointed in me?"

"You know how forgetful I am Baby. I forgot to mention this to anyone else. God only knows how much more I'll forget by the time everyone comes home."

I hugged him tighter. "I'll try hard never to disappoint you again. I promise!"

"If you do, it will be the first time," he smiled through teary eyes. "I've always been proud of you, and I'm proud of you now for trying to correct any mistakes that you think you've made. It's easy to fall; it's a lot harder to get up."

"I love you, Mother!" I said as I nuzzled into him. "Now will you tell me some lies about Aunt Sue and Aunt Allie?"

"I love you too, Genie!

Well, there was the time that Aunt Sue …"

Thirty-Two

I didn't answer any of Bryan's phone calls and managed to avoid him over the next few weeks. I even changed my cell phone number and e-mail address so that I could avoid all his texts and messages with sexual innuendos. Unfortunately, I couldn't manage to avoid all his friends, and some of them were quite cruel with their digs.

"I hear that Bryan's car needs a rear-end job. Don't keep him waiting."

"Hey Gene, what's up – besides your legs, of course."

"Hey Gene, how does it feel that yours is the butt of so many jokes?"

Sometimes the digs were even more suggestive and a lot more graphic. Obviously Bryan had been doing a lot of talking behind my back, believe me, no pun intended. I found myself avoiding all sorts of people and places in order to avoid further embarrassment. My self-imposed exile did not go unnoticed.

When Chip and Dale realized what was happening,

they wanted to call Robbie and Mark to have them try to put an end to the harassment. I persuaded them not to, saying that it was getting better, which it wasn't, and I'd rather just wait it out than get them involved. The truth was that I didn't want either of them to know anything about the whole embarrassing situation.

I don't know whether Chip and Dale had anything to do with it. I wouldn't be surprised if they did, but soon after, it all stopped. Bryan's friends and I managed to be within sight of each other, yet never speak to each other again.

There was peace. Then one afternoon a few weeks later when Chip, Dale, and I were helping Mother in the kitchen, a box of my favorite chocolates was delivered to our door with a card that simply read "I didn't forget. I couldn't forget. I never forgot ... anything!"

"Just when you thought it was safe to step outside your door, he's back!" Dale exclaimed in an evil sci-fi tone implying a Bryan return.

I was about to toss the chocolates in the garbage when I thought, "How would Bryan even know that they were my favorites?" His interest never went beyond his interests.

An hour later a bouquet of my favorite flowers, roses, in my favorite color, purple, arrived with the message, "My thoughts of you remain every bit as beautiful as your favorite flowers."

I could tell that there was concern in the room, but I assured everyone that this couldn't possibly be Bryan's handiwork. There was no double meaning, nothing lewd or embarrassing about it. Hope sprang in my heart, but I dared not give it voice. It was too much to hope for.

And finally a package containing my favorite cologne arrived with the message, "I know that you didn't tell me this, but you were wearing it on the most wonderful day of my life. I'll do my best to shower your life with all of your favorite things if I still have a chance of becoming one of them. Love, John," and, of course, his phone number.

Hope sprung eternal!

"Who is this John?" Mother asked bewildered. "I don't remember a John. You have a John?" as the twins giggled. "When did this happen?"

"I think that you might want to go into best friend mode" I said, "It's a long story. And I'm pretty sure that you're not going to want to know when or how, but I'm sure that you'll want to know John. He's a keeper, Mother, a real honest to goodness keeper. Hopefully, you'll get to find out soon enough. I can't believe it! He must have left the seminary."

"Oh My God!" Mother exclaimed. "I feel a novena, or at least a novella, coming on. He's a priest?"

I could see the scene playing in Mother's mind and couldn't help but wonder if it wasn't this God-man swooping down to carry off poor little Ganymede, or if it involved me luring the poor prelate out of his confessional by carefully dropping rosary beads along the way to some den of inequity.

"No, a seminarian! And stop double crossing yourself!

He's a seminarian, and he wasn't one more than a year ago when we met."

"More than a year ago! When you were what … Sixteen? So, now he's a pedophile?"

"Not when you consider that I lied about my age, and he was still a teenager, too."

Chip gave me a high five. Mother gave him one to the back of his head.

"But it's cool!" Chip said. "He chose Gene over God. That's certainly a high five!"

Just then the doorbell rang again. "Good God! Now what?" Mother asked exasperated. "What favorite thing could he have sent you this time?"

I opened the door to find John standing there with a worried grin. "I'm sorry! I just couldn't wait for a call."

"Me either!" I gushed, phone and phone number in hand. "You had me … actually when you had me."

He smiled. "I couldn't stop thinking about you, so I left. It was never going to work when I realized that all I really wanted was to be with you. I had to take the chance that I still had one. Do I?"

"A million in a million, and then some," I said as I rushed into his embrace.

"What did he send?" Mother called from inside.

"My favorite, Mother. My favorite."

Thirty-Three

They say that you marry your mother. I'm beginning to think that John married my Mother. In so many ways, I was reliving his life. Despite my long and continuing love for Robbie, and my obsession with Bryan, John was my favorite. I love him dearly and married him the year after we reunited, on the anniversary of our first meeting. He's every bit as accepting of my feelings toward Robbie and my family as Dad was toward Mother's feelings for Uncle Josh and the aunts. Like Dad, he understands that what's passed is past. We are the present we gave each other.

John is everything you could possibly want in a spouse. He is my best friend, the love of my life. And sex with John is still a religious experience, which is appropriate since he is now attending divinity school.

I have actually been published, and I'm concentrating on being the writer that I always wanted to be. I have never been happier in my life, and yet somehow I know that this is only the beginning.

Stephen J. Mulrooney

Robbie and Mark have purchased a huge parcel of land in upstate New York that has three houses on it, all nicely separated from one another. They plan on eventually raising a family there with help from Mother and Dad, who will soon occupy one of the houses that the twins are already staked out in.

Chip and Dale are already attending a community college nearby where Robbie is coaching and finishing his degree. I imagine that it is only a matter of time before the remaining house is occupied by Aunt Sue, Aunt Allie and Uncle Mohammed (yes, we finally got to meet him). And with Uncle Josh set to retire, who knows?

On my nightstand there is a picture of my entire family taken after John and I reunited. I stare at it and wonder how anyone can think that you can't choose your family. If there are any pictures of my family in the dictionary next to a definition, they should be next to the word "family." Each member of the chosen, and we all have been chosen, gives strength to the true meaning of the word.

I love the thought of them all together, each one a pot of gold at the end of his or her own rainbow. John is so amazing that he even talks about us settling nearby. I have to admit that I love the idea. Someday, we will want to raise a family. And I want our kids to also have the same opportunity to grow up normal.

I want them to have the love of grandparents who will hold them when they need it and tell them made-up stories to make them laugh. Who will teach them how not to throw a ball, nor catch it. I want them to have uncles and aunts who will watch out for them, have their backs, teach them valuable lessons, tell them stories about their family, hug them when they're happy, hug them when they're sad, show them how to put on shows, and wear costumes, and make life everything it should be – alive! I want them to be surrounded by all the love, beauty and magic that I have known. I want them to learn that it's not who you love that's important, but that you love. I want them to learn how to defy gravity, and to be wicked in all the right ways. I want them to know the magic of so many midsummer night's dreams that they never awaken to anything less than life as it was meant to be. I want all that and so much more for them. If that's not normal, I don't know what is.

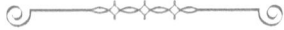

Stephen J. Mulrooney

About the Author

Stephen J. Mulrooney is a retired Employee Assistance Professional from New York who now lives in Kansas City, MO with his husband, Jerome and their canine family.

Steve's thirty-something year dream of becoming a writer began to take shape in 2009 when the characters in this book began telling him their story. It took another three years before he realized that the best way to become a writer was to actually sit down and write. It helped.

This is Steve's first work of fiction. He hopes that you enjoy this novel and the many more to come.

Stephen J. Mulrooney

Jordan Ashley Hocker

Jordan Ashley Hocker is a poet and street performer who wrote freelance poetry in the Crossroads district of Kansas City, MO until moving to Maui, HI. Her on-demand-poetry leapt off the keys of an old portable manual typewriter within seconds after a request was given to her.

The poem that follows is an exact copy of the one composed by Jordan on an August Friday night when I explained to her that I had all these ideas for writing a story, but couldn't seem to put them on paper. The next day, after rereading the poem, the dam burst and the story flowed forth.

Thank you Jordan for the inspiration.

Normal?

About: Having the inspiration.

It is something akin to
having all the toothpaste
but a block in the tube,
the moments well up,
yet the imminent release
teases and dances around us.
so hear we are,
totured to experience
all the greatness
yet to have little release.
and sometimes it is that,
there is too much to express,
when there hangs so much beauty,
how can you focus
on just one thing?
therein lies the solution,
pick one thing,
focus completely,
write a few lines
see where it takes you.
then onto the next,
not to do better or the best,
but to exercise your relation,
to limber your fingers,
to letting it flow,
to letting it go.

By: Jordan Ashley Hocker